(J)

D0358866

THE *C*OTONEASTER *F*ACTOR

THE
COTONEASTER *FACTOR*

by
David Peak

FOURTH ESTATE · LONDON

First published in Great Britain by
Fourth Estate Limited
Classic House
113 Westbourne Grove
London   W2 4UP

British Library Cataloguing in Publication Data
Peak, David
The cotoneaster factor.
I. Title
823'.914 [F]
ISBN 1-872180-60-4

Typeset by York House Typographic, Ltd
Printed by Bookcraft Ltd, Avon

THE *COTONEASTER FACTOR*

1

MARY WAKES remembering Matthew's conviction that she's never had friends or lovers, just mirrors in which to rationalise herself. It's unbearable when his voice invades her waking so swiftly and the more she waits under the covers the more his insistence on her sickness develops till she must climb out, drape the dressing-gown round her shoulders and shuffle to the kitchen, where she switches on the kettle and steps out through the back door in the hope that a quick look at the city will switch Matthew off.

They're leading extraordinary lives, that couple in the sky. For the last few days Mary's been out here before dawn to watch them, though she did miss yesterday because of the fog. Usually the dark-haired man shows up first, settling down at a table between open green curtains in the left-hand window and getting on with some kind of work till the woman wanders in from the bedroom, kisses him and makes a drink. But the other day – Saturday was it? – he was sitting there semi-naked, and when she came in he just wrapped his arms round her magnolia nightie and buried his face between her breasts. She was yawning. As they eased apart he pulled up the nightie and kissed her thigh. She made a show of wanting to slap him but then, thinking better of it, slinked at the knees, raised her arms and let him tug it over her head. He was hugging, touching and kissing her till both of them sank below the level of the window-frame, only to rise again several minutes later almost licking each other in gratitude and full of blatant coochy-coo. He was puckering for her breast even as she struggled to replace her nightie. Trickling her fingers across his chest, she put an end to it by pecking his forehead and then busied herself with some clay pots of wintering geraniums, while he carried on with his work. Whatever it is he does involves gazing into space for much of the time.

This morning Mary is too early for them, their windows just darkened hollows in a general gloom. Tuesday. Wednesday tomorrow. And while Tuesdays can be pleasant, she's not sure she wants them every week. *Christ you know it ain't easy, you know how hard it can be!* Pushing her arms into the dressing-gown and doing up the buttons as best she can, she listens to the racket of birds in other gardens and traces the unhooked necklace of streetlights weaving towards dark homes on the surrounding rise. Through a gap in the terrace she can just make out the patch of waste ground, a cream mist hanging above its pools of rainwater; beyond that, a line of railings, more homes; then more.

Still no luck. Must have overslept. Kicking the door shut she makes tea, carrying the cup in both hands to the living room where she sits in her chair to remember (invent) log-fires, hand-knitted shawls, candlelight maybe. It's like being out of time, her silence broken only by things she can't seem to have: peace of mind for example – when will that come? Taking the stained photo from the shelf she spits on the glass, wipes it with her sleeve, then lets it fall to the floor. Matthew's right about Paul, she supposes. She didn't like him at all. Ridiculous things anyway, photos. In a crimson tenderness she props the mirror against the sofa, takes off her dressing-gown and, having knelt

4

down, splays her knees. The sense of it is there and if, in imagination, she could stroke it, so it would grow; but limp like this, yes, it would be reasonably simple to stretch the tip towards its natural aperture. But what if she wanted it (laughing), really wanted it? If she was soaked and it was a monster?

Still, she'll be right as rain in no time at all, Matthew said.

There's an old tomato crate under the window where she left it yesterday, the word '*Campesina*' on its side and a picture of a Spanish woman in a straw hat holding her own basket of tomatoes under a brief blue sky. Her blouse is partially unbuttoned as if to charm greengrocers on weary dawns at the wholesale market. Beneath her bare feet is the name *Juanita*.

Hushed room as if a conductor·has just tapped his baton against the music stand. Above her is a single crimson bulb with no shade so wonderlands of shadow fall between her open thighs. Matthew has suggested she use her first half-hour for preparation, stillness, reflection; but for the second time she finds herself looking at Paul in his cracked plastic frame. *Though you didn't like him, give him space on your shelf by way of an apology.* And there he is in old green trousers and torn anorak, standing in front of a line of saplings, a biscuit-coloured church tower just visible through a haze to the left. Soon he'll tumble over the faint line dividing then and now and bother her no more – that's one of Matthew's immaculate promises: Paul left to gather dust as a sickness she once shared, their madness forgiven and he nothing more than he is now – a hump of rye-grass in the meadows of the dead.

She lies down, belly tickling on the carpet, to see her face close up. Much of the puffiness has died down, though the skin is still moist and her eyes cherish traces of yellow. From here her own smell is pleasantly repellent. Then smiles at herself, though her spirit won't join in, at a snatch of uninvited lyric… *Oh doctor, I'm in trouble (Oh goodness gracious me)*.

It would be simple with the background tedium of her mother's old mantel clock to serenade dawn with cooked-up sentiment; and, in a moment made classical by a fantasy of André Previn and regular ticking, living arrives at the point of a fulcrum, with one style this side, another on that, Mary rocking naked in the middle of it all with nicotine walls and a recent suggestion of Matthew's to make her days just a series of nows framed by sleep. And when, later, he announced a ban on her Leonard Cohen collection she laughed and he hugged her because it was one of the few times he'd heard her do such a thing. Well, she went against his command as soon as he'd left but was proven the fool because quite suddenly the old bastard did indeed ruin her soul with instability and despair.

She muffles the smell with her dressing-gown and makes a cup of coffee. Two spoonfuls, a dash of not quite fresh milk and, as prescribed by Matthew, plenty of sugar to help satisfy her system. The kitchen seems covered in grease and needs re-doing completely; the top of the cooker is still black where it caught fire and above it, on the ceiling, hangs a circle of soot held together by strands of cobweb. The lid on the waste-bin won't go down and that bottle-filled rubbish bag in the corner wants throwing out. *And if one green bottle should accidentally…*

She's stepping outside a second time and, yes, he's there now, hair ruffled, his torso billowing in a Prince-of-Denmark shirt as he bends over his work, looks up, bends down. Mary's whispering, 'Hello. I'm over here,' but he doesn't turn; looking out isn't his immediate concern. In this edge of night or day the uneven lawn and weed-covered vegetable patch are indistinguishable from each other. Paul was going to dig it all over one time; try a little horticulture – an imagined good life of wine, marijuana cigarettes, a pig for hams. And as summer crept over the coiffured lawn there would have been blue-smoked barbecues with his friends, bottles of claret, a small fire in readiness for the chill of midnight; and against the fragrant smoke he'd have admired the hornpipe silhouettes of those friends raising glasses, analysing Gorbachev, roaring backwards for humorous anecdotes or shaking heads at the cloud-flecked moon.

Arms and eyes so leaden and uncomfortable she could easily go back to bed, though Matthew has kept on and on about the dangers of it – sleeping too much and the lethargy it creates. 'Always have something constructive to do,' he said. 'But if you're really stuck then just get active. Dance. Do exercises. Anything.'

As filets of grey cloud gather at the horizon and the stars begin to fade, the man throws out his arms to yawn. Handsome, but aren't they all in those other windows? Then, from the bedroom, the woman glides to him, looks at what he's been doing and seduces his hair. They're getting along like a house on fire. As she moves away he tweaks her backside, making her jump. Laughing, he turns back to his work. She feigns a punch to his temple, then, arms like a crucifixion, pirouettes to the back of the room.

Strictly speaking, Mary should draw up a plan for the day but figures it would be a pleasant change to have time off from planning; to just wait and see what comes along. Besides, Matthew's ringing at lunchtime to check up on her, so that's a handy point of action to live round. Waving anonymously to the couple up there who are now both at the table, foreheads touching, she steps back into the kitchen, swills her cup, takes her vitamins, brushes crumbs from the cupboard, then turns on the immersion for her umpteenth bath. She prepares a second coffee which gets cold as she's straightening the damp bed-covers, gathering used tissues from the floor and emptying the hot-water bottle. And she must go round to the launderette some time. Then there are Paul's clothes to get rid of. The smell of them is everywhere. Maybe she could drop them off at a charity shop. Maybe not.

Waiting for the bath she drinks half of the cold coffee and turns on the radio. News is still a source of open-mouthed entertain-ment to her because somewhere along the line she's missed out on several 'international incidents', as they're called, all of which would have bothered her had she been conscious of them. Now she's been advised to listen once a day, and adds the crises up, making bets over the outcome, though she's helpless to influence the millions either way, and when all's said and done she has only that stack of washing and an envy of Paul who no longer cares. Not that he ever did; he can't choose now whether to suffer or treat things with indifference; has only the sleep of sleeps and his space in the photo-frame, white hand tucked round the handle of his plastic bottle-bag. In his background, the tips of saplings are about to break into leaf. Here are fragments of his inebriated dream – a spring countryside, a quiet stroll through the wood. And though his smile has fooled a few, Mary's untouched. She shrugs her shoulders

She's scuffling through for another peep. The man's stopped working and serves with a spatula what look like mushrooms on to what must be the woman's plate. She reaches for her knife and

fork, merry, beautiful as anything, light brown hair over magnolia shoulders. As soon as he's finished dishing up, the man
stands back, spatula and frying-pan held apart as if to say, 'Into
your hands I commend my spirit.'

2

BATHTIME. She'll not bother with the flannel, just ease back and let the water swill these mounds and crevices. There's no allowance in Matthew's philosophy for basking in this way, but she'll do it all the same. Even with life as the reward one can't be forever vigilant. A second silence has fallen; not on this wet level but further down in the wreaths of spirit. Playing a game of undulation in which nipples, pubic hair and the dream of it dink above the surface, plunge back, the water clouded with bath-salts – a present from Matthew just the other day. Meant he couldn't stand the stink, most likely. Now she's slipping fingers through pubic hair till she's whoops-a-daisy, then more hot water. She deserves it. And Paul, well, he won't be beating at the door to blaspheme this luxury with a bout of his throwing up.

Yes. Running from the tennis courts one evening centuries ago down soft garlic-green lanes of church-bell and blackbird. Peter had broken his racket in temper but came to see the funny side of it as they reached the police station at the end of the lane and poured into the village high street.

'Shall we go to the Crown?' he asked. 'I bet old Harry'll let you have one.'

Old Harry did. A glass of lager. It was an evening of sunlit trees, pastel hillsides swamping crooked roofs and beige pavements; then that crimson bar with mugs of shadow, Russ Conway swanking in the background. Through the quartered window above Peter's head she could see a black wrought-iron gate leading to a garden where pink-suited children were playing on a rusty swing. Either side of the garden were cottages with rippled windows and studded front doors. Beyond a wall at the back lay a composition of lilac and apple-trees, nut-coloured fences and, just visible but broken up by leaves and branches, the grey gable of the Tudor manor house. Peter was swivelling his pint mug. 'Yeah, good bloke, old Harry. Doesn't mind you coming in as long as you're quiet and toe the line.'

She was realising how tall and innocent he was, his head skew-whiff as if he'd been born too quick and cricked his neck against the bedpost. Jaw red with precocious shaving; fair hair from his fat German father; and he was claiming to adore her, though with blue eyes rather than words, thoughtful fingers rather than direct action. The village a carnival of quietness, and of its four pubs this one was the resting place of escaped prisoners-of-war and stiffened men in patterned trousers who drank large gins and whose hounds, on what-ho mornings, tore foxes apart.

Peter would have wanted to end the evening with an unexpected holding of her hand and a walk, perhaps, through sinuous cotoneaster roads to the quarry-top where they could snuggle against the stars and listen to the scented vale, its screech-owls, wood-pigeons, crickets. It must have been him who sent her the transcription of 'The Cloths of Heaven', and maybe he was hoping a few lagers would soften her opinion of him. He was playing games with his beer-mat. Old Harry polished wine-glasses at the bar.

Coming home... Peter with hands in his pockets, the finest slice of moon hanging between treetops and stars. He was talking to Mary on the corner by the chemist's, though he'd long run out of anything decent to say. On the opposite corner by the sweet-shop a pair of harmless bikers on growling machines revved up after whistling at a pair of giggling pretties dressed in blue. The village was hemmed in by its hills and there were memories everywhere, going back, oh, donkey's years, to acres of fat bramble, haunted barns, vine-tangled copses. The fragrance of it all was bringing her a rare contentment as Peter finally said, 'See you tomorrow?', waited for a contradiction, then, hearing none, strolled diagonally into Fox Lane.

Fine day. Playing tennis late afternoon on courts at the back of the admiral's house. The rolled ash surfaces lay in a man-made hollow surrounded by tall Scotch pines. At the far end, in a pouch of honeysuckle and lilac, stood the old green pavilion, leaning to one side in much the same way as Peter's head. The pavilion was empty but for a small baize-topped table full of woodworm, a book in which to sign your name and numerous lace cobwebs lilting in the angles. In between sets Peter liked to sit on the rotting verandah with his can of shandy, ticking her off for winning so often, the Ken Rosewall racket wedged between his legs. As a crimson sun slipped among the pines, the scents of evening hung thick as dust through the greens and shadowed blues of woodsmoke and rhododendron.

She was walking home beside the line of somnolent cottages (each with its yellowing net curtains and nameless old woman) rehearsing her excuse for being late. Reaching the gate she could see a faint light hanging from the window of her father's workshop. Her mother, pulling herself steady in her chair, will have rattled the side of the glass with that noose of a wedding-

ring, peered at Mary to assess degrees of guilt, then welcomed
her.

'Oh. So you're back?'

Stepping down from an intangible dock, Mary pecked her
mother's blue hair and escaped to her bedroom, where she sat in
the window, listening. Above the orange tiles of the outhouse lay
an arc of sky patterned at its lower edge by the tips of trees and in
its upper reaches by a dust of stars. Below lay a dark garden
surrounded by a bluestone wall, minimally illuminated in one
corner by the lamp in what her father called his 'doghouse'. He'd
be out there for another hour at least. Then, the lamplight
dying, he'd stoop into the garden, pause to inhale the stars,
padlock the door and thump to the house, the empty Marilyn
Monroe glass swinging from his fingers.

Sometimes in Peter's parlour on analytical evenings they'd play
Bridge Over Troubled Water and he'd be there, crushed against the
dark rose wallpaper, hands tucked behind his head to keep it
steady, eyes closed. In the right light one effect of his blondness
was the impression of a lack of eyebrows. On his parents'
drawleaf table stood a green glass bowl piled with oranges and a
permanently unopened bottle of Advocaat. A thick maroon
curtain covering the door kept out draughts and, from his
emphysemic parents' point of view, muffled the overactive
rhythms of 'Baby Driver'. He wouldn't own up to sending the
poem; preferred that she should glean the truth by his closed eyes
and the sublimity of the music he played. Perhaps he wanted her
to lie by him, nuzzle her head against his blue shirt or kiss his
twisted mouth.

No. She hasn't bothered with the flannel and eventually climbs
from the bath, weak with heat, drying herself with an off-lemon
towel before going to bed, pulling the covers up to her chin,

tugging the stained pillow round her ears and struggling for comfort, knees up, one hand caressing her breast, the other tucked between her legs. Her smallest finger soon moistens. The fragrances of yesterday have seeped into plasterwork, floorboards, these indelicate blankets.

Asleep on and off for twenty minutes, and in that time the postman pushes a gift catalogue through her door and the milkman, hopping from his float, knocks twice but, getting no reply, takes it upon himself not to leave any milk till the bill has been paid. Upstairs, in the first-floor flat, China girl puts on her tights, skirt, white jumper and black low-heeled shoes, then sits at the dressing-table brushing out her hair. Immediately below her, pink and reasonably safe, Mary rolls from one dream to the next while the world beyond the window grows weak and green with damp sunlight flapping at singed honeysuckle curtains tanned by months of cigarette smoke.

China girl is the most beautiful of them all, more so for her natural modesty, gentle ambition, grace. The brush she's using is part of an old dressing-table set with inlaid mother-of-pearl. Bowing her head, the black hair reaches her lap and hides her face. She pulls the brush through it, over and over.

Mrs Charles next door, *that* way, owns the whole house, tee-hee, since her husband's death, so she drifts and wallows among chimes of silver and a gluttony of plush upholstery. She pulls at loose skin on the back of her hand and calls to a Pekinese who died a month or so back. You can hear her sometimes, weaving from room to room and crying, 'Sebastian! *Sebaaastian!*' And next door the other way, in a neglected house without bell or knocker but with a large number painted clumsily on the door panel, live six or seven students with a room and sound-system each. The road beyond their smeared windows is grey-green and secret with parked cars, someone else's litter and an abandoned grocery store.

In the twenty minutes, Mary wakes several times, but only for long enough to acknowledge whispers from other gardens, the sound of a car horn or the scream of a baby. She dreams or thinks of Matthew and his warnings about what he calls 'the old terrorist', who he believes will go all out to recapture her, especially in these vulnerable early days. She'd been quite helpless with this information, then heartened slightly by his smile, thick spectacles and baggy red shirt. And always the twinkle in his eye like a star guiding wise men; a star risen from the exhilaration of having outwitted his own old terrorist for so long. Holding her shoulders he shook her once and said: 'Don't worry. Do the right things. And if you're ever tempted, pick up the phone. Trust me and you'll be fine.'

And oh at the time how nice it would have been to have had a little fucking instead of medical advice.

Though she doesn't remember waking, she's lying on her back smoking the stub of a cigarette thinking of this freedom, being intimidated by what disciplines it might entail. The stub could be the remains of one of Paul's last cigarettes, soiled by his purple lips shortly before he tumbled towards his you-know-what.

Relax for now. Imagine a light waterfall against you. Listen to China girl singing as she gets ready for work. Then maybe go for a walk, keeping in mind what Matthew said about choosing a goal before setting out, otherwise she might find herself wandering aimlessly, shipwrecked by agoraphobia. The curtains billow into the room and there's one of those birds whose simple song

15

sounds like a lorry driver whistling at schoolgirls in the street. A
January bird. Yes, choose a suitable landmark, press on till you
get there, rest for a moment, then come back. She's playing with
her right nipple, squeezing it between yellow fingers, and there
isn't a surface in the room not covered in dust, cup- or bottle-
rings, or strewn with irrelevant objects — an old John Smith's
Yorkshire Bitter can on the dressing-table, in the middle of the
floor a broken umbrella, four empty record sleeves. As usual at
this time of day she wonders what it is people do and why they do
it, taking China girl as her main example, who leaves for the
bank regular as clockwork on weekdays, body quickened and as
finely sculpted as a China girl's should be.

Sometimes on those old mornings there would be great bright-
ness and she'd play Cat Stevens, then crawl back to bed to catch
perfumes through the window. Her father wasn't the sort to say
'Cheerio' before he left for work. In the garage he had an ancient
Ford Popular up on bricks and whenever her mother got the
better of him he'd go and caress its torn leather seats and bumped
black bodywork, then come into the house not quite sure what to
do with himself, saying to no one in particular: 'One of these
days I'm going to restore that old car.' Her mother had a familiar
joke then, whereby she'd look out of the window for flying pigs.

Pillows grey with grease, sheets crinkled and generally damp
with sweating. Sometimes she thinks of herself as a sponge in the
process of being wrung out. Slipping from the bed she looks
through the curtains at those windows in the sky where the man
is working and the woman stands just behind him arranging her
hair, turning down the collar of a blue blouse, then looping what
look like pearls round her neck. Letting the curtain fall back,
Mary stands, legs splayed, in front of the wardrobe mirror and
bends to touch her toes. But what if some sneaky guy should

come at her from behind? The Lone Ranger. Tonto. Or both? Faintly yellow and moist all over and Jesus said, 'Consider the lilies of the field,' but then He would, so she stands to attention sideways, stomach pulled in, shoulders back and her breasts aren't bad at all if you ignore the dark hairs surrounding her nipples, not that anyone's likely to be taking mouthfuls in those regions for a while – the 'terror and bewilderment regions' as Paul called them. And she can't help fingers roaring through her thighs till the image of it stiffens. Without it, she's something of a Looby Loo, but the sensation is distinct and quite unarguable. Standing frontwards, knees bent slightly and arms thrown up as Jerri Hall might, she tries to picture it ... but then, a little bored, she shakes a finger at the mirror, snaps herself away from it and pulls on her knickers. How long's that now? Four, five days? Paul didn't care because he'd usually had his on for as long as that. Pick people with the same sickness as yourself and it hardly shows. She remembers Matthew leaning against the doorframe saying, 'This place stinks.'

She managed to whisper at the time, 'Charmed, I'm sure.'

Somewhere, in among all these homes, Glen Campbell's singing 'Wichita Lineman' and she's recalling an evening at that girl's house – what was her name? Anyway, something like Michelle. Peter was there. It was supposed to be a party because the girl's parents were away in some country or other lunching with diplomats and in the living room, as Glen began *I am a lineman for the county,* the three of them were engaged in an honesty session with Pernod as a tongue-loosener till the girl threw up most of her dinner across the Wilton. Peter cleaned it up, then took her on to the patio for counselling, leaving Mary in the arms of a bottle and her special cigarette. Through french windows a summer night soon sang, immaculate with stars and jasmine.

Peter came in to apologise for his absence but he was having to wash down the patio as well and by now he stank of aniseed. Later the three of them sat together saddening over James Taylor till Michelle, or whatever her name was, crazy like the old Frenchwomen with their absinthe, climbed on to the coffee table and took off her clothes, challenging Peter to touch parts of her body. He simply fell into the night with his glass and wept for a time on the orange swing-seat. Michelle jumped to the floor and lay lengthways on her back, incoherent and somehow never less naked, her eyes avoiding Mary's as the night wore down.

By now Mary's wearing her matted dressing-gown, watching through the living-room window as China girl skips down the steps, a white leather bag hanging from the shoulder of her black coat. Matthew believes the most important thing is to take recovery one day at a time. *Don't go regretting yesterday or rehearsing tomorrow.* She grasped at his incantations because they'd been the only ropes dangled to her while she drowned. By this time of day, a while back, her guts and head would have been yelling for it, but then, once she'd given in and calmed down, she'd have been able to call herself an average person with, OK, a few nervous problems (who hasn't?) which had to be kept in check somehow. And since doctors asked too many questions and were patronising bastards anyway, who could have denied her the right to that personal solution? Who?

Still January. A pair of women along the road in cracked brown shoes and coats the colour of seascapes. The dazzles of sun are like flames across the window opposite where the hint of a figure stands well back in the shadows of its room. She scratches a tickle in her pubic hair. (Those tiny creatures like dinosaurs through electron microscopes, munching pieces of a tastier world.) Yawns. Perhaps she should make a list of chores and tick them off as she goes along rather than charging at them like a bull at a gate. Not that she would. Tablets have taken away any hoorays for sticky streets being waded through by those not minding, well, reality. She can still smell herself, despite the bath, her armpits already wet and that autumnal smell... Yes, mushrooms. The same perfume after all this time. And what her mother would have called her 'water' leaves much to be desired – she daren't breathe too deeply while she's passing it, bright yellow now as well, what with vitamins and this other shit. *Had I the cloths of Heaven...* And there's no point bothering with her hair when it'll just end up the same and the same.

Lifting the hem of her dressing-gown to show knees, thighs, stroking the skin with her fingertips till, oh, she casually tickles it and snaps at her breath. The hem falls. No one out there anyway, except for the figure far beyond the burning window. She curls on her chair reading 'Laughter, the Best Medicine' in an old *Reader's Digest* but soon throws it to the floor and stands up. No one understands her anyway. She's rubbing her nose with the nub of her palm; then, even though she hasn't planned it, puts her thumbs in her ears and waggles her fingers at the photo of Paul. As usual, the part-conjured sequence of events comes to her: Paul with Billy the Boot at someone's party in a flat high above the street, both pissed. Paul dancing to Tracy Chapman, then either tripping or throwing himself through the window; somersaulting once (some said) but, anyhow, falling the last few feet, legs thrown apart till he was impaled by Georgian railings. Flailing his arms and head (others said) for several minutes, then going limp like a dead sparrow, witnesses running in panic or pretending nothing had happened, and even the first ambulancemen (according to rumour) threw up over reddened flagstones.

3

COLD TURKEY. Matthew was looking after her that first night, sprawling with a magazine on the sofa or standing at the window sipping coffee till, round three o'clock, she began to hear the movement of birds in the bathroom and though he was telling her it was just an illusion created by a disappointed brain in league with the inner ear she couldn't quite bear the sound and broke into an unstemmable sweat. He held her hand and told light-hearted stories of himself. Both he and the room became agitated. He was lighting cigarettes for her as the room danced and she did her best to keep it steady by gripping the chair, but repeatedly the walls swung away and the air thickened. His deep voice was here or there, in the next road or from the heavens, while far below dark choirs sang, *Like a circle in a spiral, like a wheel within a wheel...* A dissemination of the world and its familiarities. She was saying, 'Can we try this tomorrow when I've had more time to think?' and Matthew was laughing, not at her, he said, but at the memory of himself saying similar things. He reminded her that just a few hours before she'd made him promise not to listen to any protests she might make. As he was speaking she wanted to run away, but she was wearing her dressing-gown as a precaution against this and he had rounded up all the money he could find. In the worst of it he phoned for a doctor and she was hating him for sticking so rigidly to his promises and herself for having the gall to ask them of him in the lagoons of an earlier tranquillity. Her eyes were out of control. Fists tried punching their way out of her gut. She shook till she could barely speak. Heaved over a bowl, bringing up a watery bile. The doctor came, gave her some medication and left a prescription for Matthew to pick up in the morning. Then she was trying to read nice books in the hope of finding niceness herself, but each imagination of an end to withdrawal proved premature and she ended up pacing to the bedroom and back over and over, unable to get warm or comfortable. Just before dawn, with the help of medication – of which she took an extra dose while Matthew was in the bathroom – she fell asleep. At eleven or thereabouts, he woke her with sweet coffee and further medication from the chemist's. Half-way through the afternoon, when she was beginning to think she had it cracked, she threw a convulsion. Matthew, having seen it all before, was there, absolutely there with his teaspoon and cold flannel. She took some convincing that the convulsion had happened. After all, she couldn't remember it.

'Of course you can't remember it,' he laughed.

She sort of laughed too.

Sunlight through the living room, draping the chestnut sofa and its companion armchair in beaten green gold and picking out individual brush-strokes on the woodchip-paper walls. Matthew would be disappointed if he knew she hadn't dressed yet. She'd argue that remaining undressed was one of the temptations of her convalescence, finding pleasures in skin when nothing else can bring them, enjoying the immediate tickles of loose dressing-gown over gooseflesh. In the kitchen she prepares a snack of soft crispbread and a rubbery triangle of old Edam; stands in the sunshine to nibble at them and sees that both the man and the woman have temporarily vacated their windows, though they've compensated for this in the left-hand one by placing a vase of dried flowers on the table. And it's too much; all of it. Letting the dressing-gown slide to the kitchen floor she's stepping out of her knickers, throwing her arms towards a proscenium arch and shouting: *'Hey! Big spender.'* The last man (if you don't count Paul) was Billy the Boot and what a fiasco that was, him pissed anyway and angry as hell afterwards, blaspheming her as he pulled up his damp jeans, then cracking the dressing-table mirror with the back of a chair. Still shouting at her, he clumped up the hall in his high-heeled boots and stole a ten-pound note from the table. For a while she lay on the bed charting the progress of his warm semen as it trickled down the inside of her thigh to the sheet, wondering, but not seriously, if there was anything deadly in it. So pissed had he been she couldn't get out of her head the image of those sperms doing a Tiller Girls kick and singing *Roll out the barrel!* Then she half-decided to go to the launderette to swill Billy out, but Paul was labouring on the motorway extension and she remembered she was supposed to be minding their stall at the market. She'd been going less and less because even at that time the person who'd turn out to be Matthew would watch her from the market café opposite as if he knew something she didn't. And she grew angry with his eyes. Now and again she'd decide it had all been a figment of her imagination, but then she'd spot the café lights flashing on his thick glasses and find herself unable to pick up her cup or move about the stall with any conviction.

And the wider you throw your legs, in this naked condition, the more immaculate it feels and you could dance before thousands the rhythms of this rhapsody.

I could show you a (Boom! Boom!) good time (Boom!).

Then at school, when winter and mock examinations loomed, Bruce came to teach maths and she fell for him in the way girls do. Despite a certain reserve she'd gaze at him in lessons or hang around afterwards with the other sillies to ask questions she didn't need answers to and he was tall and sinewy, *interesting* rather than handsome. You would have said he had a fine sense of humour, manifesting itself in a collaborative cynicism over his own subject, those symbols and figures, logarithms and the thighs of youngsters blooming. At the bell he'd toss his piece of chalk into the audience, and rap his fist on that pile of books. 'Well, there's another hour of your life taken up, for what it's worth,' he'd say. Married with a boy child and living on one of those frail Sixties houses down by the library. One afternoon she came across him while she was walking through the woods, so they talked for a while about schoolish things – him, you know, acting the father, but then starting to tease her, cracking what you might call *suggestive* jokes and pinching her waist till he feigned to stumble down a grass slope and pulled her with him and the expression on his face changed from father to angst child and he was pulling up her jumper, unbuttoning her blouse, nibbling her young nipple. There were hopeless numbers of rooks crackling the woodland and she remembers him saying: 'There's something in you, Mary, which sets you apart from other girls,' which she thought a fairly smoochy thing to say and by then he was lying with a cigarette explaining how his wife and child were away for a week visiting an ill parent in Leeds, so he took her home (when it was dark) to show her some badly coloured magazines and super-eight movies and, while apologising for how rotten he was *going* to feel later, did it to her on the sofa till there was a general commotion and the sod Pythagoras didn't seem to come into it and Bruce was engaging her in trick-filled conversations in which he loved replying to his own questions while she lay, dimply and sweet as a youngster should.

23

Oh he loved generous measures of gin mixed with Vermouth only he called it Vermooth and both of them laughed a lot over his way with words and the maladjustment of Peter's spinal column. Then, kissing her dimply sweetness he came to believe he loved her. She'd been a virgin if you didn't count fingers or Milky Ways, and he came straight back with, 'Ah, the sweet you can fuck with between boyfriends.' Hearing himself say this, he came to love her heaps more, brushing his lips across that milky abdomen, those tiny breasts; told her in the hot dark how he'd noticed her the first moment he walked into that first lesson; how he'd loved her eyes and thighs, and she said, 'That rhymes.' On another day he brought her, funnily enough, to this city to see *Hamlet* the play and Hamlet the person and they had drinks at the Printer's Devil afterwards. No, he wasn't happy at home because though he was fond of his wife she was so… How could he put it? … So negative, and generally didn't like sex any more, at least not the *adventurous* kind, and besides he'd sensed an intrigue brewing between her and that garlic-breathed bastard Wilkins from Nineteenth-century Social and Economic History. But, yes, he did love his child to pieces and would never abandon him come hell or high water and, no, Mary couldn't get pregnant because he'd had his tubes snipped and he told stories of a domestic woman in green overalls who'd been in the room while he was having the operation done on his whatsit, which was poking through a hole in a large green sheet, and when he'd seen it lying there, as it were, isolated, he'd realised what a mystical thing it was, not that the quietly guffawing domestic shared his opinion.

Of course Mary didn't dare reveal the scandal to her parents, so she invented a more appropriate boy from school to explain her behaviour. The invented boy's name was Alexander and in her fantasies they had quite a time of it, poring over scrolls in the library, examining wayside flora. Soon she had a lengthy but fictitious biography for him – how his mother wore turquoise hats and his grandfather had shrapnel – but most of all she loved the bit she'd slipped in unintentionally about him being allergic to butterflies. In many ways this relationship was more satisfying than Bruce, who veered increasingly towards fuse-changing and other domestic excuses. *(I'm gonna do all the things to you a girl wants a man to do, oh baybeeee.)* Unfortunately her mother, glad to hear of some male friend without a deformity, became quite fond of the fictional Alexander and began to invite him home for tea, whereupon Mary was forced to kill him off on a fictional holiday he wasn't having in the Algarve with his non-Great-aunt Sarah. For a few weeks afterwards she went to church to give credence to the lie. Meanwhile (take a deep breath) the return of Abigail (Bruce's wife – small thing with long limbs and that look of lined beauty and gratitude often visible in maths teachers' wives) meant a redevelopment of what little behaviour was left to them, so they met once a week (if that often) in the pavilion at the back of the admiral's house but only when moon and temperature were in synchronisation and only then for a short time – time enough to work up to sex, down from sex and, in between, have it, with no words and an increasing clenching of the teeth on Bruce's part. There came a night when he didn't show and at school the next day he left the room before she had a chance to speak, so she phoned against instruction but his wife answered. In the background she could hear the television and the chatter of a playing child. Some evenings she spent walking up and down his road glancing at his windows, themselves illuminated by the blues of the television, but she only ever saw the top of his wife peering, as it were, over the battlements of marriage. A few weeks later another teacher took over and Bruce went away and a film of grey settled over early spring and the grey wouldn't shift, lingering right through a soft blue snowfall in April. (In the mirror now, she's laughing over the absurdity of it, arranging her hair and flattening breasts against her palms.)

Matthew was leaning forward, gaslight dancing on his glasses. He needed to put across that, though she naturally wanted to examine some of the things that had happened to her long before, she shouldn't fall into the habit of attributing *blame*. Wisdom was gathering in furrows along his forehead.

'When the old terrorist comes,' he said, 'he doesn't have a motive, but all the same he'll try to persuade you otherwise and you'll end up with some fairly sound rationalisation for your difficulty and those in turn will justify your actions if you decide … well, to go back. You must sweep away the ruins of the past. [Mary laughing.] We're not meant to *use* our imagined tragedies. Do that too often and you'll be a dead duck, believe me.'

'Very good,' she said.

He cleared his throat, adjusted his glasses. 'Of course self-pity's the one to watch. It kills. The only important thing is that you're here now, this minute, and you have to find a way of going forward with different attitudes. If you look back, say, and decide that things were a bit darker after incidents like this maths teacher business, then you should think of it that the terrorist just took advantage of a common situation. In that way it's easy to see there's no point whatsoever blaming the present on the past. Quite frankly I'd say, fuck the maths teacher.'

'I was thinking much the same,' said Mary.

Sun shines across the room, forcing shadows to tuck in corners; somnolent rhythms through the thin walls from next door. It's a mild winter of light and greens and primroses – symbols of the beautiful but always *over there*. She's rallying just a fragment from the crispbread and cheese and dances to inner rhythms in partnership with glimpses in the mirror of pale skin, veined breasts, a slender neck, chin held high. She should exercise, he said, but whenever will she find time for this monumental list of things to do? And which should she begin with?

A sigh like the exhalation of a god – it's a balloon coming over the rooftops, blue, red and yellow, a silver basket hanging beneath and those specks of the brilliant few, waving. Doing a ballet round the living room, as she turns, she catches sight of the ruined Lautrec print, an empty packet of joss-sticks and, next to it, the torn beige scroll of Desiderata and she's remembering Paul in one of his more finely balanced moments of inebriation stomping back and forth crying out in mock German: 'Go placidly 'midst the noise and haste and remember what peace there may be in a slug of Johnny Walker.'

Bathroom. Thighs flattening on the black seat and they are never less attractive than when doing this. Holds her breath through-out. Wipes herself with a piece of newspaper. Pulls the flush. There's evidence of her greasiness in the bath, where scum has become attached to an adhesive waterline. It has claw feet. Paul almost sold it to Billy the Boot, and though Billy came round and was very tempted he rightly concluded there was no point having a claw-footed bath but no living quarters to put it in. She's yawning. A yawn that follows sleep, an unquenchable tiredness to dog her day, frequently persuading her to sit down or curl up on the stained floor-cushion. She gets dressed. Billy the Boot stank of cider. It was one of the ways you knew he was in a room or one of the ways you knew *he'd been* in it. The ginger hair curling over his chest, then gathering into a narrow thread over his white abdomen till it reached his groin and spread again. It'd just happened that she'd been in the underpass on her way to the market but couldn't work out how to get home. Billy the Boot spotted her and offered to escort her home, his colleagues jeering as he took her arm and half dragged her up the blue steps to the street. 'Brilliant bit of skirt. Like to fuck you rotten,' he was whispering, and, at the flat, he did just that, promising to be swift in case Paul came back early. That's when he got angry and stole the ten pounds. Later, when she made the mistake of coming clean with Paul, he said he'd go straight out, find Billy the Boot and thump him for thieving, but somehow he didn't get round to the thump bit and the next day she saw the two of them leaving the Paradise Lost, arm in arm and singing, *Oh soldier, soldier, will ye marry me, wi' your musket, fife and drrrum!*

4

WALKTIME. She's pushing the front door closed, green winds brushing her like conciliatory palms and the figure in the opposite window skulking round curtains as if its imminent death is her fault. There's reggae from the house next door, the singer Caribbean with an orange drink and calypso shirt and, yes, it's an ozone-deficient but pleasant day, sky soft with woollen clouds slipping among these multiform roofs. She's chosen the castle as her goal, four miles away on its conical hill. Paul once did a balancing act on the battlements and she remembers saying, 'Mind you don't break your neck.' Coming out of her road, turning the corner into the street and she's quite certain she'll over-breathe among this mismanagement of signs, indicators, shoppers and crack-bottomed men in yellow trousers drilling into the road then hacking at fragments with spades. Irish trousers. And to gain confidence she's singing *if dogs run free*, though she always forgets the words after the first line and, anyway, since the beginning of this supposed 'getting better', Bob Dylan's just another one who can't communicate. Oh, his voice may be the same but somehow this new universe doesn't suit him and the *heart* seems to have gone out of him till he's just a bad poet with laryngitis, no more a prophet of the times than the Duchess of York with her stock-cube dresses and freckled good afternoons. Mary's passing the

amusement arcade, its darkness thick with truants and paedo-
philes, a lasagne of bicycles on the pavement outside and
wherever she looks there are businessmen with handkerchiefs
not-for-mucus tucked in their top pockets, and later they'll all be
in the Pig and Peacock, now open for most of the day so the
afflicted – as Matthew would call them – aren't as evident as they
used to be. There are plenty of places for them to shrink in dim
crimson bars among circular tables and those fruits flashing on
the gaming machine and with a win it plays an addictive tune so
you walk out humming, like Paul once did, a hundred pounds
with just ten pence, and he came right on home with a
presidential smile and something special from a friend of a friend
of Billy the Boot. For the next few days it was just Paul and Mary
and a benevolent outlook on this kind world and its brilliant
peoples, and they saw no end to it; an investment for a long
honeysuckle future. But Matthew reckons living's a bit like
taking out a bank loan – you have to pay for it eventually. For
Paul it was the day a week or so later when he went into the Pig
and Peacock with eighty pounds and came back with just ten
pence, crying in his chair at dreams gone topsy-turvy because he
didn't have anything for his mother's birthday other than a limp
charity card showing 'The River Avon at Evesham in Spring'.

A glimpse of herself in the insurance office window. *Just look at
that hair.* And though Matthew has said there are plenty like her,
the road is full of capable personalities and she's not sure he's
been telling her the absolute truth. She walks close to buildings
on the right-hand side, turning frequently to see how far she's
come. A sunburnt man with a scar stops her to ask if he's on the
right track for the gymnasium and she replies: 'Yes. Just carry on
for a hundred yards and you'll see it on the left,' though he won't
because it's at least two hundred yards on the right. There's
nothing for her to enjoy in passers-by and, anyway, she won't see

him again in her lifetime (if she has one owing to her) and it's making her realise just how many dispensable people there are. She supposes she must be one of them. Moments later the man comes puffing to her side.

'You wouldn't fancy coming along with me, would you?'

She agrees with him.

'I mean, I don't do this normally. Ask strangers. But we could stop by for a drink.'

'No thanks.'

'I'll make it worth your while.'

She smiles and walks on, with him hanging back damp and over-developed in his royal blue tracksuit. Some people you come across in the street manage to concoct beautiful scenarios in silent parallel to what they're actually doing which is nothing more than *passing by*. Mary smiles, despite flutters of agoraphobia which in turn prompt an acidic nausea. Looking back, the street is winding on and on till it's obscured by trees and blue and biscuit walling. Singular events are poking through this sea of hers, but there's no way of knowing whether *this* is connected to *that*. She's walking against inclination and in spite of the weight of hands, one at her throat, the other at the back of her head. In the road beside her a sweeping man sits on his empty trolley smoking a cigarette while immediately above her a woman hangs a bed-sheet out of a window, the wind catching it till it's just a dream gone blossoming. *Oh that this too too solid flesh.* And there's a sense of softness between the pavement and her shoes. He said it repeatedly. *There are others just the same.* She scrutinises everyone for signs of it. 'I know it won't feel much like good fortune to begin with,' he said, 'but you should thank your lucky stars you're here at all. It will all get better. I promise. 'Till then she should move deliberately into the eye of the storm, head down, teeth clamped together thinking *Keep at it* or possibly *Hi De Hi*.

Yes, she was walking down a narrow footpath between slopes of firs, Peter in front, the field-glasses thumping his chest, a thin sky of steel-grey and soft blues against which he caught the antics of a lapwing or the panic of a pheasant pumping upwards from the undergrowth. The flowers of bluebell, wild garlic and herb robert hung between rust-coloured trunks as a fine mist, and as leaves and needles closed in around the path so the perfumes thickened, exhilarating him. Twice he stopped, lay his arm across her waist and said, 'Listen,' but she could hear nothing except in some sense the plump silence itself. Through breaks in the trees he was watching the silver meadow and, beyond it, a further ridge patterned by the blossom of hawthorn and the iridescent greens of unfurling plane trees. In the distance, suddenly, the soft insistence of a cuckoo and she was realising how close to *now* he was and envied him since other matters kept shielding her perception of it. Where the path reached its lowest point adjacent to the meadow and began to climb again, they had to pick their way round a mess of puddles and mud churned by horses' hoofs. A little further up, the track was surfaced with beige stones and the firs were interlaced with young beech trees. He stopped again, saying of the beech leaves, 'You'll never see a green as green as that,' and she was getting angry at his pleasure. He was soon sitting on a sawn trunk where he had a wide view of the village, the undulation of its journey down the escarpment, its bloom of chimney-pots, the lime dust of its church tower. His legs were thrown open and where they began to cower in the shadows of his campfire shorts they turned delicate, pale, more personal somehow and she sensed that if ever anyone were kissing his legs starting from the shin, something in that higher delicacy would sadden them. He was half humming, half singing *and it seems to me you lived your life like a candle in the wind,* while Mary sat likewise opposite him.

On the second morning of her recovery, she woke with wet sheets. She stripped the bed and had a bath, flannelling herself till her skin turned red. On the mattress lay a stain like the pattern in an onyx paperweight, ever-lightening rings spreading outwards. Her limbs itched from the inside; eyes a kaleidoscope of blues, maroons. Matthew arrived early, just as she was dumping the sheets into the bathwater. She was hating the precision of his experience and would happily have replaced him with someone to whom she could lie, or at least present a more reasonable image. There, in her dressing-gown, talking nineteen to the dozen while he sat on the sofa with a cigarette, listening, she prayed he wouldn't be with her long enough to want to visit the bathroom, but her prayers weren't answered. Coming back into the living room he simply put his arm round her, squeezed, and said he'd make coffee.

Reaching the park as an intermediate sanctuary, its gates open and, as usual, the first sight is of those rain-rotten toilets (often home to Billy the Boot), the damp rubber-seated toddler swings, almighty leafless beech trees and geometric areas of grass enclosing malt flowerbeds and pruned roses. She's sitting down but it's not easy to hold on, as if the park will swing upwards and leave her dangling from the bench, shoes towards the fathomless sky. These, so *he* says, are the immediate legacies when you lose your comforter, each just one sideshow in a carnival of senses. As he said this he was watching her with love, though he was quick to point out it wasn't an *afternoon* love with Tanita Tikaram or the intimate consumption of plum-jam sandwiches. Just love. And he was saying something like he'd do anything to help providing she wanted to get better.

She pulled up her chin. 'And if I don't?'

'I'll just come back when you do.'

'Ah, your concern has strings,' she said.

He laughed. 'No, it's not like that. You'll understand as time goes by.'

She aimed at him through one eye. There were moments when it was as if he'd recently clambered out of an article in *Reader's Digest*.

The park's a rage of movement. She's holding on to the wrought-iron end-frame of the bench and would give almost anything for these sensations to stop though she understands that the only thing capable of removing them promptly was probably responsible, as Matthew claims, for creating them in the first place. And these aren't people in the ordinary sense of the word – in macs and overcoats, hurling sticks for their dogs or walking for walking's sake – but interlopers from some other world intended to highlight her ineptitude. He reckoned these early days would be full of similar moments, and just when she thinks she's about to go mad she should hold on. Exactly that. Hold on. 'And anyway, aren't these feelings a jolly good reminder of what it's all about?' She laughed at his 'jolly good' but he didn't see, or wouldn't allow himself to see, the funny side even when she tried to explain it to him. Her left hand grows white as it grips the bench. She considers making do with having come this far. Perhaps an eight-mile round trip had been a little grandiose. Biting off more than she could chew. She takes a tablet from her pocket and swallows it, believing that for some it must look a glorious day with its smooth blues and the slightest tips of daffodil shoots poking through the grass. Or perhaps turning back would be Matthew's concept of *copping out*. Her dreams are interrupted by a scruffy woman swanning along the path on unsteady shoes against a background of a rippled city. Some would say Mary is as ragged as the old woman and that her spirit somehow resides with this unformulated soul in its torn dress, soiled bloomers and most likely those nests of crawlies between the legs, and if you asked the old woman she'd maybe sing, *Wrong? Nothin' wrong wi me lovey. Piss away wi yo.* Mary grinds her teeth. Drums her fingers. And at the very tip of a cone of vision, a particle of wanting and a sadness that at some time or another she'd been optimistic rather than cynical. What happened to that? Houses round the park are eyes with their focus on her, making her stand, yawn, behave as she imagines she would if she were an ordinary person, re-tying her shoelaces, snapping fallen twigs, watching youngsters on swings. Then she's following the outer path of the park, close to the railings, hunched up, and she'd like to cry, spill some unknown out, let the cat out of the bag. Coming to the top gate she leaves the park, follows the blue road till it reaches the railway bridge then takes a short cut through the allotments, coming out by the stream and the derelict mill where that friend of Billy the Boot shot a cat then shot himself, her panic softening slightly as she passes the primary school where it's playtime, boys looping girls with maroon scarves or waving fingers at Mary, all of them giggling with milk, hymn books, statistics about the Veldt, that beauty in the horrorplace, blacks sliced while whites clap, the earth a rumtiginous place for sure till a swept-back woman with Olive Oyl shins snaps into the playground and shakes a brass bell. The clatter may beat Mary into a corner, shatter her, push her over some kind of boundary. She's thinking of warmer things, long summer afternoons, house martins skipping through the blue, the puffs of rhododendron blossom, and yet each of these is sinister in itself. She's gripping her fists, stamping forward, beating it out. There's a prayer Matthew advised her to use in last-resort circumstances but she can't remember it, doesn't believe in God, and even if there is one it must irritate him no end to have set phrases thrown at him day after day like trying to make love by reading a manual so, rather than wallowing through the stars, you'd be simply obeying the instructions of page 123, 'How to Do It Properly'. He said she should try the prayer anyway because it works and many's the time, he said, when he's been wandering through the shops whispering it to himself. *God give me this that or another, oh, and half a pound of mushrooms.* She's walking beside the army barracks wishing she wasn't, a neat dark green man with stripes standing by the guardhouse with an alsatian.

At the market one cold December lunchtime she was on her stool drifting between one thought and another, tapping her foot on the waste-bin (in which each snack she'd bought from the café for the look of the thing lay neatly wrapped in pages of a *Radio Times*) and trying not to watch the café window where the man with thick glasses was examing her with more vigour than normal. On her table was a plastic cup she couldn't pick up. Soon the man came out of the café, looked up and down the aisle, strode over to her and leaned into her life, his forearms squashing against the table.

He cleared his throat.

'Look, I know you.'

'Oh really?'

He half smiled. 'Yes. I think you've got … a problem. And it's scaring you stupid.'

She was reaching for her cup but stopped just as her fingers touched its rim. 'And what problem might that be? Other than you watching me all the time?'

He adjusted his glasses. 'Well, if you don't know then I've made a mistake and if you do I don't need to tell you.'

She squeezed the edge of the table. 'Anyway, what gives you the right to march up at people like this?'

'I don't suppose I've got one. I'm Matthew by the way. I didn't want a long conversation. But here's my phone number

and I'd just like to say that if things, well, if you decide ... just
ring me.'

He brushed her hand lightly before pulling up his collar,
rearranging his glasses and walking away. She watched him go.
The market became unbearable. She arranged the items on her
stall, arranged them again. Sat on the stool. Stood up.

Coming from an alley beside the scrapyard she turns left into the
wide main road behind the green hypermarket which continu-
ously releases people with too much shopping into a geometric
precinct from where they must flow through a subterranean
walkway and emerge into a large car park, sunlight catching
their raised boot-lids and abandoned trolleys. And though she
isn't cold, she feels surrounded by a wall and over that wall
trolley-pushers sing in the sun while she hauls breeze-blocks
through snow to raise grey buildings with concrete floors, the
grit of each block skinning her fingers. And somehow self-pity,
though a state of mind frowned upon by Matthew, is by far the
sweeter thing, sweeter in its way than the radiance of others
who'd be saying, *Look, the day is soft, the sun shines, we are each in
the ascendant. Be content.* She's climbing into the walkway, its
tiled walls repeating each step; tiled side-tunnels each with its
musician, criminal, disappointed opera-singer, and in the lowest
point of the main tunnel an old man holds a broken guitar and,
behind him, sellotaped to the wall, there's a hand-written notice
beginning 'Peoples of tomoorow. I aand I the sons of...' An
upturned hat at his feet holds sixteen pence. As she passes he
strums his fingers over three strings.

As soon as she was physically capable, Matthew took her on a
tour of the streets, showing her the latterday crazies in their
cardboard bedrooms, those snatching dreams from wayside
benches, those still living it up with a jiggedy two-step in

memory of Ginger outside the Pig and Peacock, and he had with
him an invisible almanac of well-thought-out phrases. 'Here you
see proof of the insidious epidemic, Mary,' he was saying, though
it was hard to believe he wasn't just some drop-out from a
Jacobean theatre company. 'The disease with a smile on its face.'
Each time something like this sprang from his lips he'd watch
the pavement and shake his head. She was close behind, being
asked to follow in the wake of his convictions. And as their tour
continued he related in more detail incidents from his past: the
severed relationships, violence, spells in prison; then his moment
of awakening, decision and eventually *peace* – not happiness; at
least, not as he would have imagined it. Peace was more
substantial, something he cherished; something which calmed
him on both good and bad days.

'It must be lovely for you,' she said.

He kicked an empty fruit-drink carton into the gutter. 'Don't
talk like that,' he said. 'Don't disown possibilities. What we're
trying to do here isn't unreal, unusual or anything. It's just
putting living to rights. Remember that? Living?'

'How do you spell it?'

He turned to face her. 'Every time I say something serious you
brush it off. I think at some point you have to face facts and join
the human race.'

She noticed he'd said 'join', and not 'rejoin'. Yes, that's what
he said. And it's because of him she's out in this thick nowhere
and won't be back before he's due to ring and he'll probably
spend the afternoon looking for her, but as always it will be an act
of self-improvement on his part rather than some heroic rescue of
her.

'After all,' he said on that same walk, 'I can only hold on to
this miracle by giving it away.'

And despite how close to death she was feeling she leant
against a telephone box and laughed into her hands.

Some time during that summer, or perhaps it was earlier, her father decided the family should move away from the village because he was bored with its stillness and tired of driving back and forth, and anyway it would do everyone good to have a change of scene. Her mother wept for several days. On their last evening, as Mary was tucking herself into the window-seat to watch a large crimson sun sink into the trees, Peter came to say goodbye, spending an hour or more on the floor by her bed gazing at the walls and window, his lips out of alignment. A room softening to the smell of stock, a tang of fried onions from the kitchen and that sense of the brown-sugar earth. Peter, as if he were about to catch a train to another country, reached out towards her, waggled his jaw then came to brush her cheek, whispering, 'Sorry,' as he twisted away again. He was wearing black shoes, grey socks and his beige shorts.

Mary had said a kind of farewell some days before – to the emerald valleys, the pastry-coloured village with its church tower, thatched cottage, lily-covered duckpond; farewell to the shorn lower slopes of the escarpment reclaimed for sheep and buttercup cattle; to stereotypical hip-injured farmers in large wellingtons, their bellies swollen with mutton, their varnished cheeks cracked through whistling to sheepdogs; and then memories, a chaos of them – cracks of willow on the village green; long conventional afternoons by her satanic stream; the lanes draped in leaf-shadow; the white mansion where Lady So-and-so hanged herself; the mortuary now converted into a bungalow; old men sleeping off rough cider in hedgerows; women squeezing fruit in the high street; the church on green evenings throwing its chimes through a hundred indifferent windows; Peter's father with his brass spittle-pot; the pair of greys reaching over the wall of their beech-cooled field; proud men coming home with bean-poles cut from the ridge. And as she was performing this ritual of farewell she realised she didn't give a piss for any of it and would mostly enjoy its somnolence in retrospect.

Then, reaching over, Peter touched her leg. But there was no danger in him, which is why he would go on to lead a barely inflated life. It had taken one of the last puffs of his courage to roam her shin then wander upwards, but he was stalling in those realms of thigh and looking out at the brightening stars. Three times he fumbled, three times apologised. Eventually the offending hand was tucked tight between his knees.

'Oh, I'm such a prat,' he said.

Her father's chosen house was an end-of-terrace in a cul-de-sac with a crazy-paved area at the front and a large garden at the back, in the corner of which he built himself a wooden 'dog-house', planting a commemorative silver birch beside it. The view from Mary's window was brought up short by a line of houses beyond the garden. She stared out at other windows and those windows, flashing with leaves and narrow skies, stared back, day after day.

Along Harlequin Road, by the swimming pool with its intestinal waterchutes and, to her right, a row of squat houses and a derelict church, its pointed doors pink with graffiti and its prophets of stained glass locked behind a rusting mesh. On the road itself a slap of hazard lines separates the traffic, one or two cars tooting at her, making her jump if not in skin then in soul, and at intervals everything slows down, backs up all the way to the roundabout and drivers tap their steering wheels or run a comb through their hair. Her throat dry, hands wet and legs somehow forgetting to remind her when a foot is due to reach the pavement or a knee might find it felicitous to bend. And rising above the middle-distant houses, the castle, ancient on its conical mound, thick and impenetrable to sentiment. The immediate vicinity is crowded with unknown persons standing in cafés with cups of tea, queueing at the fishmonger's or sitting on benches. These hideous tasks such second nature to them when for Mary walking's enough, quite enough, because these shoes sponge into the surface of the pavement and in these wild dreams there are dribble men slinking in toilet doorways to suffocate her for tuppence. A large junction, several sets of traffic lights, a bank, old folk with demented umbrellas. It's like this, Matthew. Waiting for a chop on the neck or a burst blood-vessel or this stomach about to cast out what little content it possesses. Her legs without bones. She's crossing the junction, on the lookout for whatever-it-is; windows, one storey, two, three, puce curtains, the face of a dog, an old man's ear pressed against the glass, the fingers of strangers waving, the flick of hats, of shoes, of neon café signs and perhaps, ha, she could lie down and let them smother her in kisses, let them dabble in moist pastures, let them stroke her – stroke her to minimise differences. Or she could stand here in the midst of it shouting, *I can't deal with this ordinariness,* and hope that someone, just a little someone, would concur. And who's kind? An ambulanceman perhaps? He'd be kind. But even then it would be as if each kindness had a devilish intent, as if his uniform hid hoofs and horns. (It's half-past nothing in the desert of her day. *'Desert'*, not *'dessert'*. A dessert's something with hundreds and thousands you eat with a spoon and as you lift the spoon it goes Squawk! like trifles on television and the worst of it is people buy them because they go Squawk!, not because they taste special or anything like that.)

One of the most symptomatic things is letting your mind run away with you as if you lack the natural barriers to lunacy taken for granted by others, these others, these hundreds and thou-

sands unaware of your ... well, suffering ... though it's not useful
to use the word, so Matthew says and he should know, but even
he loses empathy at a certain distance down the road of identifica-
tion. Yes, she's seen him nod at what she's said, though there's
often a trace of discomfort in his eyes. It can all be brought
about, this sense of imminent peril, by a word, gesture, sound,
let alone when you're in a street heaving, as this one does, with
people busying to and fro without time or consideration and
though you might dream of there being *some* consideration even
the thought of *that* could drive you into a doorway where you'd
curl up, melt away.

Then a second afternoon, a day or two after Matthew's proclama-
tion, and she was in the market café thinking over what he'd
said, her coffee a fine cocktail because her gut was in a mess and
she'd been troubled for some time by a putrefied taste at the back
of her throat and a stink similar to it in everything around. At
the café window, the face of the person who'd recently opened a
shrub stall, peering in, his hands either side of his head like
blinkers. Michael, was it? Methuselah? Certainly not. Martin –
yes, that was it. Martin. He was opening the door, adjusting his
jacket, walking in spotlights to the counter where he ordered a
coffee, glanced at her, came to stand for an abject few seconds in
proximity to her table then, pretending to spot her, dragged out
a chair and sat down. He was scrutinising her damp face. Placing
a palm over her plastic cup, she glanced at him. He winked.
Jerked his head to one side. Smiled gradually.

'I love you,' he said.

'Excuse me?'

He was examining the pepper-pot. 'I love you.'

Turning away from him a little, she sipped her drink.

He replaced the pepper-pot and picked up the tomato
ketchup.

'Sorry,' he was saying, 'but I've been waiting ages for an opportunity to present itself and, well, I saw you here all along and I decided to come out with it now while I had the courage. (That's a nice jumper you've got on.) Anyway, there was something in my bones telling me now was the best time. I've been a bit bothered because you don't seem to have been on your stall much lately and the days you weren't there were, well, like lifetimes.'

'I think you've mixed me up with someone else.'

He was pointing the tomato-shaped plastic ketchup bottle at her. 'No. It's definitely *you*.'

Yawning, he sprawled back in his chair as if the unburdening had tranquillised him. She took frequent sips of her drink to abolish the taste in her mouth. 'You must be mad.'

'In one sense yes,' he laughed. 'In another, well, no.'

'But you can't have seen me more than a couple of times.'

'Yes. It is strange, isn't it?' His absent squeezings on the bottle were releasing a blob of ketchup. 'Still, I don't suppose circumstances alter facts. Here I am and I love you to *bits*.' He grinned and shook his head. It was as if the café had silenced itself to listen in. 'And that's more or less the whole story. It's probably a bit of a shock. I can see that. Thing is, I have to pop up the lane for a loaf. Do you want to come?'

She came.

She was following him along the sparsely populated aisles of the market into the narrow lane where the banks' and solicitors' windows were billowing with cold and there seemed to be an inordinate number of women with blue hats, men with bowlers and rolled-up umbrellas. Martin was just in front of her, humming, patting his pockets, turning to her if he needed to wink, and at her breastbone a persistent gnawing, an uncomfortable compromise between starvation and nausea.

'Beautiful day, isn't it? My favourite time of year. Things have such a, kind of, romantic melancholy, don't you find?'

She had moved into the shadow of a church to rest against its wall. He had walked another dozen paces before he noticed she was no longer behind him. He turned and came up to her.

'Look,' she was saying, the wall behind her swaying a little, 'I don't want to ruin your day but I'm sort of with someone already and if he saw you acting like this...'

'Oh, *him*,' he said. 'Sorry, but I'm not worried about that because, I mean, I don't think you like him. The few times I've seen him I've thought to myself "Well, they aren't suited for a start." I sense things like that, don't you? Anyway, come on, let's get this bread before someone walks off with all my plants. I asked the vacuum-cleaner man to keep an eye on them, but you know what he's like.'

The flagstones beneath her shoes were growing increasingly unstable and she was resenting his ability to negotiate them without a second thought, the blue wind catching his light brown hair and a smile about him visible even from the back. Reaching the bread shop he went in for his loaf while she waited in the shadow, tapping her shoes against the grey stone, watching the narrow strip of sky and a motorised hang-glider crossing it. Around her the click of Tuesday heels. In the shop, Martin leaned against the glass counter laughing with the sales assistant as she wrapped his bread in tissue. And that stink again, faint but somehow more distinct because of it. A man and a woman were passing by, the man saying in a Yorkshire accent, 'It's the jackpot this week, Mavis, I'm sure of it.' Mavis replied with a flick of the eyebrows in a world of benches with tuna sandwiches and the jangle of the brass bell as Martin abandoned the bread shop and came up to her, laughing at himself.

'For a moment in there I thought I might come out to find you'd been just a figment of my imagination. Do you do that? Think that things you've been enjoying might be figments of your imagination? Happened to me yesterday in the super-market. There was old Anne Diamond buying custard powder. Well, I came out of there wondering if it had been ... well, you know, a figment. I waited outside but I didn't see her again. Life's like that, isn't it? Wondering if so-and-so was really Anne Diamond buying custard powder.'

Mary had found an empty bench and was sitting down, wondering if she might be sick. Martin collapsed beside her with a rapturous sigh, the lane and the fringes of the market a symphony of colour and movement.

'Know something? I've had my eye on you since... Well, *since*, and the heavens (if there are such things) seem to be decreeing that you're instrumental to me and I haven't yet doubted the truth of it even when you've looked as if you were, sort of ... having a bit of difficulty with yourself. I think it's in your eyes. Sadness. A look of having to put up with something. Who knows? Perhaps I'm here to help you in some way. Maybe that's what destiny has in store. Fairly exciting, isn't it?'

She caught her breath and swallowed. 'You're an arrogant person, aren't you?' she was saying.

He smiled and twisted his loaf. 'Some would agree with you, but then I've been figuring it can't be wrong, can it? Loving you. Sorry.'

His laughter was running resonantly along the flagstones as her sense of consciousness rose and fell away. Opening the tissue he plucked a corner of crust from the floured loaf and ate it.

'Well, this is nice!' he was saying. 'The sun's lovely, isn't it? And everyone looks cheerful today, though that might just be me. Have you ever had one of those days when people look sad but then you find out it's your own sadness kind of colouring them? Well, it's the same with cheerfulness. Something nice like this happens, and quite suddenly the world's well, gay, I suppose. And here we are. Sunshine. A beautiful bench. Enthusiastic streets. And you.'

Beneath the taste of the back of her throat was a sense of deadening, like the after-effect of a cough mixture, and her hands, as they twisted in her lap, ruffled the air somehow and there was that smell coming from her clothes and perhaps he'd caught it on his senses and had come up to her to all intents and purposes like a dog, tongue lolling out. And yes, way over there, in a thick of people heading away from the market she saw Molly, or the unmistakable back of Molly, and she wanted to turn to Martin and explain: *There's Paul's old romance.* But there was no point, given that Martin didn't know the first thing about *her* let alone old acquaintances. And she was remembering Paul and herself on the physio steps doing it for the first time and how afterwards he'd told her about Molly. 'But don't bother your head over her,' he'd said. 'She's pissed off with me anyway. Probably be fucking glad you've come along.' And so she was, coupling up with some guy called Leo and becoming, according to Paul, 'fucking respectable'.

Martin was coughing to gain Mary's attention. She turned to see him happy as a waxwork. He winked again. She winked back.

'So what have you got to say about all this?' he asked, slapping his bread.

'Nothing very much. Sorry.'

'Nothing?'

'Nothing.'

'You mean you're not...?'

'No.'

'Not even in the...?'

'Not a bit. I just want to be left alone.'

He was running a finger between his collar and neck, then rolling his shoulders. 'Yes. That's interesting. Tell you what. I'll go back to the market and give you a chance to think.' He was standing up, waggling his bread by holding the ends of the tissue till it gave way and the loaf fell to the flagstones. He picked it up, waving to reassure passers-by as he did so, then made unsuccessful attempts to wrap the bread in the torn tissue.

'Well. Thank you for listening to what I've had to say. I hope none of it has disturbed you and, well, perhaps we'll have a chance to talk again soon.'

Adjusting imaginary sword and cloak, he strode away, turning to look at her but pretending he was turning to look at other things. Once he was out of sight she grasped the end of the bench and climbed to her feet. The lane was turning golden and there were groups of people laughing at the entrance to the market. Reaching the toilets at last, she pushed two fingers to the back of her throat.

She's walking through an area of the city which is strewn with wholesale clothing warehouses, converted cinemas, and small turban shops where – if circumstances necessitate – you can purchase a puncture repair outfit *and* a haddock, and beyond them on concrete stilts the motorway threads its way above crouched terraced houses, the remnants of its vibration somehow under her feet. To the left the castle dominates from the top of a hundred or so steps hewn into the hillside, the thin atmosphere of the streets below thickened with its release of phantoms and by its grey shadow; phantoms conjured through centuries of sameness; and there must have been a time when the castle looked across abdomens of meadow, bleak hawthorns and rivulets of

winter, but since then it has witnessed the tapping of one brick
on to a million others, the swing of axes and the unrolling of a
broad concrete carpet.

5

CLIMBTIME. She'll make a commitment, as Matthew suggests, to wait two minutes once she's reached the battlements before coming away. Getting better is about repeatedly facing what scares you, he said, though it's a difficult business all the same. She's remembering Paul up there, clowning around, waggling his arms in mock loss of balance, and oh, the serenity of the castle walls on that particular day, Billy the Boot slumping to one side with a grin on his face. But then the next night she was woken by the sound of Paul pissing in the corner of the bedroom, turned around to see a moonlit hint of his underpants wedged into the crease of his backside and she was hating him, maybe because he was a symbol of herself, but at least she'd never done *that*. Listening as it struck the wallpaper and ran to the floorboards. He was holding himself up by pressing one hand to the wall, his head bowed in examination of his own process, thin legs whitened by that same moon, and as usual when he did this she pulled a blanket from the airing cupboard, dragged it into the living room and curled up on the sofa, leaving him to fumble with the honeysuckle curtains for an access to the bed. She remembers thinking of Martin and his parcel of bread as she lay there in the stink of a world gone twisted and unreasonable and if she'd had a shotgun she would have pushed it against Paul's guts and pulled the trigger because she was sick of how white he was, his smell, and that inability to be reasonable. From the bedroom came the sound of his howling, which had become the mark of him when pissed and semi-conscious. That's what he did – howl towards sleep. Then, hours later, with birds sipping puddles in the garden, she awoke to the music of his retching as if suddenly his intestines would break from their moorings and gallop through his mouth in an unbroken tangle, blood-red, sweetened by webs of mucus. Maybe his spirit was coming up too. Directly above her she could hear the paddings to and fro of China girl and see, through a gap in the curtains, the figure of that elderly person in the house opposite, swathed in a saffron dressing-gown and sipping tea from a Chinese cup. She remembers thinking as she listened to those footfalls above – such a ridiculous thing – *China girl, I love you,* and could suddenly recall in one sweep every time she'd seen her coming light and full of song along the road, carrying shopping or a book or a bunch of flowers; and all the moments her black hair had been captured by the wind and sun or flattened into rats' tails by a burst of rain. China girl, the beautiful one, nothing to tarnish the images she'd given rise to. And Mary with dreams of China girl's looking-glass, collecting the reflections of black hair brushed in the mornings, the crinkles of nose as she inspected her own features or the gentle applications of eye-shadow. Yet there was and is something in China girl's sweet competence which irritates Mary. Probably she would refer to her as *That woman downstairs. The bitch with no self-control.* Mary on the sofa, hair wet with perspiration and a pillow stinking of mushrooms. That's right, Paul came in, wiping his mouth with a towel.

'Lousy stink in the bedroom. Probably that fucking tom-cat again.' Then he threw on his bottle-coat. He'd promised to meet Billy the Boot to talk over a deal and later they were going to a party. 'Reckon we're on to a winner if we can get the bread together. Are you gonna spend the rest of the day on that sofa, or what?' He poured himself a drink from a bottle on the table, threw it back in one, then swung out of the room, slamming the front door. The window rattled. Upstairs, China girl, perhaps choosing a blouse then slipping it on, tucking it into her black skirt, would have been the scent of musk with a sweetness of skin at her thigh and warmths you could tuck your hand between. Mary imagined them celebrating together, China girl's teeth chuckling against the rim of a glass.

She's climbing slowly upwards while high above a line of heads peer through the battlements and binoculars flash towards the horizon. Weak and breathless, Mary turns around as if to enjoy the view, remembering the city when she first came and how its howl wouldn't stop. She would watch night across unfamiliar gardens; the moments in other windows of women in dressing-gowns, men Windsor-knotting ties, couples preparing intimate suppers; then the rare but beautiful movement of one nakedness against another, lights on, curtains forgotten, lifestyles on cinema screens. She took to turning off her own light and watching through her father's binoculars, creating names and imaginary dénouements for those she saw. She liked to join them, in principle at least, by standing tight to her own dark window, daring herself to undress. Almost the whole purpose of clothes is to anticipate removing them, though there was often a sadness in the final garment, prompting her to want them on again. But she loved to resist the temptation to conform, enjoying moonlight on her skin and roomlight on other skins or girls in pigtails, friends arriving with a bottle, dogs jumping up in welcome, spaghetti being poured from a saucepan into a colander, youngsters jigging to music through headphones; and waiting there against the glass she'd run fingers along her shoulder, down her arm, over breast and abdomen till she ached for things she had no names for, fingers along the outside of her thigh, tickling just above her knee then, if the mood bloomed, resting in an armchair directly in front of the window, her legs thrown open and her favourite peacock feather taking the place of fingers, its tip slipping along the inside of her leg for the benefit of those, perhaps, with binoculars looking her way. Music. She still loved Cat Stevens then. Feather like a bow across the strings of a cello, less soluble darkness temporarily forgotten. And, if she was lucky, a tumbler on the window-sill and the mumble of uninterested parents in the room below.

The sun is warm against her back as if spring's a temptress come early to deceive and, out of breath, she sits to one side of the steps to look across homes, factories, railway lines, scrapyards, the city dumped just here in the crook of the hills, its ecclesiastical and historical buildings brushed clean on the skyline over there and thousands of windows, many of them throwing out second suns over a grime and quietness not worthy of them. And if, as Matthew says, these physical symptoms will easily recede, then what other barrier is it she must lift to let in a sense of *being here*? It is relatively simple to see that such and such is beautiful, but she would prefer to *feel* rather than to know. She's too light and might float away from the hillside or too heavy and could sink beneath it, hands on knees, chin on hands and it's the smell of mushrooms, without a doubt. Sometimes it would be good to run away, leaving yourself behind. Coming down the steps, some are arm in arm, are the boop-boop-dee-boopers – those she couldn't explain any of it to with much success. And what to think next? The locomotive of imagination coming up against buffers and she's had this thing about steam trains but no experience; *this thing about steam,* jumping down from a railway carriage to an unknown platform, a suitcase in her hand; a sense that she could choose where to go and how to get there with nothing to dictate that choice. Now the denim's tight against her thighs, and an urgency (if that's the word) pushes against the undercrease of her jeans as she swings around and climbs to her feet, the castle rearing backwards in retaliation. She'd like to be fondled by the population of China, since experiences of that kind have a tendency to subdue psychosomatic symptoms, leaving you with what's actually wrong. The effervescence of her gut pushes against her bowel here and the entrance to her gullet there and nausea reaches into her fingertips.

'Mary?'

A voice from the battlements but she doesn't look towards its origin since she has been caught like that before – making the mistake of thinking every hailed Mary is herself. But as if conscious of this argument the voice calls a second time.

'Mary!'

An arm waggles in the sky. And whereas she would like to turn and retreat, the rule must include getting right to the top, otherwise... But then, isn't it ridiculous to create difficulties in such simple things? The things others would pooh-pooh. Matthew argues that this preposterous state of affairs comes simply from an obsession with self. 'At some point you'll live without perpetual reference to how you appear in terms of everyone else,' he said and at the time she would have said, if she'd had the voice, 'I'm deeply grateful Matthew for this information now kindly piss off.' Reaching the last steps she hauls herself through the portcullis and enters a narrow doorway in the turret to her left. Once upon a time men stood around here in metal suits thinking they understood everything. Had no cause to wonder whether their Vauxhall Cavalier was safely parked. Once driven, forever a smarmy bastard. And within the turret a darkness of ghosts, the cold echoes of ramblers moving up and down and among them the voice: *Mary, are you there?* A chorus of youngsters cheering. She's squeezing past figures coming the opposite way, catching up and overtaking the terminal lungs of an old woman till she reaches a rectangle of sky and battlements. In the midst of it, a wriggle of blue and grey folds its arms.

'I can't get over this. It's actually you.'

She's walking round him to keep her appointment with the battlements. He's following her.

'When I got up this morning I had a feeling I'd come across you if I, you know, waited here. And here you are. Large as life.'

'Somewhat smaller, actually.' She's leaning forward only to be thrown back by the vertiginous view. Martin grasps the next battlement along.

'Couldn't believe it at first. Well, people have hunches, don't they? But you don't expect them to come true. To be honest, there have been quite a few times when I've thought I've seen you before but it's always been wishful thinking. So till you walked out here I wasn't absolutely sure. You OK? You're a bit pale.'

'Knackered, I expect.'

An ambulance scatters traffic in the road below.

'Honest. You're washed out.'

'Haven't been well. But I'm sort of on the mend.'

'Good, I'm glad.'

She has already sensed it – this gladness of his. He's a glad person thinking back gladly on the one glad time he has had with her.

'Thanks.'

'Love it here, don't you? I love old things. Having a lot of past is almost as good, in a way, as having a lot of future. And I like thinking of a time when people just *were*. Know what I mean? If someone came along they didn't like, they just fired an arrow at them and that was the end of it. And when a king or whatever galloped over the horizon waving a poll-tax leaflet, you tipped boiling oil over him. You didn't have to go through all this democracy stuff. Democracy's just subtle dictatorship, isn't it? Hey! That's not bad! I keep meaning to write these ideas down. *Democracy's just subtle dictatorship.* It just strikes me that the government always goes ahead with what it wants to do whether you agree with it or not. Personally I'd love to capture a few of them down there and boil up the old cauldron. They'd be looking up screaming, "But we've got a mandate from the people," and I'd pour the oil at them and scream back, "Well you haven't got a mandate from me, you bastards..." Oh, sorry, I hate bad language but there are times when it fits in so ... well, metrically. Right then! Now you're here, how about a coffee in the Castle Cafeteria?'

(He's the very model of a modern Major General.)

A little further along a young boy drops his toffee-apple over the battlements, counting as it falls.

'Well, I...'

'It's a nice place. I had a quick one earlier. And do you know what? I saw Valerie Singleton going in as I was coming out. Brought back all kinds of memories.'

As Martin gazes at her, the landscape rocks from side to side and nausea scampers half-way up her gullet before losing its grip and slipping down.

'Yeah, remember? John Noakes acting the goat. *Get down, Shep.* Made me sad when I saw him replace old Ted Moult in those double-glazing things. I kept thinking, "John you should be scaling chimney-stacks, not doing this." ' (He's shaking his head.) 'All that rigmarole of dropping a feather down the window-pane. I tried that myself once. Have you? And do you know something, *my* feather went straight down even though I haven't got double-glazing. That's the trouble with advertisers today. I've read books about it. They create a sort of paranoia in people about feathers, and everyone goes out to buy the double-glazing without realising their feathers would probably do all right anyway. And then there's all that toothpaste nonsense. When people get bored with any particular brand the manufacturers come up with another deadly thing in your mouth the toothpaste will cure now they've added something with strange initials. I mean, I hadn't even heard of plaque, had you? Then suddenly everyone's rushing out to get the stuff that cures it. Sorry, but it's one of the bees in my bonnet. I expect you have them – bees in bonnets. Do you want a coffee then? Sorry, but I'm in one of my chatty moods.'

Touching her shoulder momentarily, he walks to the turret door and she's following him down the steps to the echoes of his narrative. From the bottom of the steps he guides her across the inner courtyard to a kind of greenhouse she can't remember seeing before. Inside the greenhouse there's a jungle of tropical plants and, among them, chessboard tables and a clutter of excuse-me chairs where beefy men search their heads for hair and argumentative pensioners sedate themselves with Lapsang Souchong and listeria-free chicken sandwiches. Mary must sit *there* while Martin queues at the counter with his dangled tray. She has a good look at him. Jeans too tight. Probably has to lie down to get them on. Yellow paint-stain on the back pocket. *(Isn't it rich? Aren't we a pair?)* Shirt dangling below the hem of his grey leather jacket. Hair shorter than last time. Slightly sticky-out ears. Fairly attractive till he opens his mouth. Movements awkward, as if apologising to strangers for his birth. He's noticed her watching him and waves to her. And, OK, he wouldn't hurt a fly but there are people who won't hurt flies because they are genuinely reverential to every creature on earth and others who won't hurt flies because they want you to think they're the reincarnation of St Francis though secretly, when they get home, they splatter them with rolled-up *Suns*.

Nasty little creatures. She was coming awake one morning on the sofa, wetness through the padding over the springs, and she couldn't recall having seen Paul for a while. In the night she had woken several times and the one dream she remembered was of children being liquidated in the Near East with machine-guns. Wet yet again, and as usual she was seeking other explanations for it and for the stickiness between her legs till, with an ensuing wakefulness, the fact dawned and wouldn't retreat. *(There ought to be clowns.)* On her way to the bathroom she was crying. Such a response didn't occur often, but she gave in to it this time, slamming and locking the bathroom door, crooning towards the mirror and trying to smile but calling herself a bitch. There was no hot water. The pot containing a dead cactus had somehow contrived to slide down the enamel surface and scatter its dry soil around the plughole. Upstairs, China girl was playing a Phil Collins thing about love gone up the creek and Mary was sitting on the toilet applying shampoo to her pubic hair and thighs to take the stink away, though soon her spirit was catching fire as she dreamt of it rigid in her fingers, the lather becoming thick and cool, a fine lubricant in its own right.

The Castle Cafeteria rocks, cheerfully at first. Mary, the numb centre of it, picks at the undersurface of the table, jumping at the rattle of cutlery, clatter of cups against saucers, the murmur of conversation. Immediately next to her a couple lean towards each other though their glances part just as they are about to collide, the woman fiddling with the tip of her little finger, the man sighing in an effort to prompt conversation, and in between the condiments sits a volume of Proust and, beside it, a second book with a large photo of a marmoset on the front cover and, above it, the title *Marmosets* in purple. In spates of glancing at them Mary realises that the couple are in offensive collusion, wanting to be together but fighting it away. It's something in their attitude and their eyes, marmosets and Proust beguiling the issue of love.

And yes, battling with it, by heaven. Battling. There's a sense in which love, once conceived, should not be pursued if it's to remain perfect since pursuit leads to erosion. And whatever it is between these two, it's much larger than either of them, which is why she's fiddling with her fingertip and he's playing with a piece of tomato on his plate.

Martin weaves between the tables, the tray in his hand, and he's bought her a sandwich, thinking she may have been deceiving herself when she refused earlier. Ham. Strips of its fat hang from the edges of the bread. He unloads the tray with some exhilaration.

'I've been thinking about it and I reckon that's what makes England *England*. Not just the usual things like the boat race, Wimbledon and Test matches in the rain but people like Ted Moult. "Old Ted Moult" I've always called him and I think that if you end up being called "old" someone or other, then you've cracked it somehow. "Old Kent Walton", there's another one. He's cracked it. You might forget about him most of the time, but England wouldn't be England without him. And it doesn't really matter whether the psychopathic shepherdess goes on for another decade or not, she won't stamp out the characters that make England, well, a place Mr Kipling would be proud to live in. The cake Kipling that is. Not the "Boots boots boots" one. I don't know what you believe in, but I think I have less respect for the psychopathic shepherdess than anyone I've ever ... well, not *seen*, because I haven't seen her. Yes, that's what I call the old despot – a psychopathic shepherdess, beating at the sheep with a dozen crooks. Here's your coffee.' He's sitting down, leaning towards her. 'And when I turned round at the counter just now and saw you sitting here, it was one of the best moments of my life. But don't worry. I'm not going to get heavy. Now. You have to tell me everything. We didn't really get round to finishing our last conversation, did we? But – without wanting to trample your wishes – I don't, well, want this one to end so abruptly. How have you been getting along?'

She's scooping the froth from the top of her coffee with a spoon and tapping it into the saucer.

'Oh, just fine. You know. Dying, but generally tip-top.'

'And are you still with that, er, other chap?'

'No.'

He's shaking the oblong sugar-packet before tearing the top. 'Well, there's fate for you. Here you are quite alone and, well, here am I. I've been keeping a close eye on the world since I last saw you and, well, I … I was worried to death when you disappeared from the market. "Martin, you're sunk," I said to myself. To be honest – and I don't want you to look upon this as your fault – I only stuck it out at the stall for a week or so after you left. I'll probably go on the dole again. It's not too bad except for the queueing up on Monday mornings with all those black labradors and people with orange hair, and having to go for those, whatjacallits – Restart Interviews, after which you never do. Re-start, I mean. In the one I had last year the woman kept asking me what I was, you know – meaning what did I do. And I kept telling her I wasn't anything in particular and she got really shirty. Well, they do, don't they, when you're *not* anything? On the form I had to fill out I put "Martin" where it asked "Normal Trade or Profession". Yes, I can be pretty rebellious at times, but I have to be in the right mood, unlike, say, Malcolm X, who I should imagine was in the right mood most of the time.'

(The man at the other table reaches across to take the woman's hand. She gazes at the connection, then looks at him. He's saying, 'What I've been meaning to tell you all this time is…' He leans back, lets go of her hand and watches it retreat under the table into her lap. Then, taking a deep breath he's coming forward again till his lips almost touch her hair. 'I'm wildly in love with you. That's what I've been meaning to say.' The woman watches her coffee cup.)

Martin has adopted a look of adoration and sympathy, held stoically till the idea strikes him to consume his sandwich, which he does with deliberation though, being normally a very audible chewer, he keeps his lips closed and his head facing slightly away from her. As soon as he's finished he dabs at his lips with a tissue and, without a word, buys a second coffee. At her request, he eats the unwanted ham sandwich.

('Wildly? What do you mean, wildly? What's the point of sticking an adverb at the end of every declaration you make? Do you know what I think? I think you're hoping to alienate yourself from the common run of things. Why can't you just love me? After all, it's what you do, not what you say that I take notice of. For a start, even though you're saying you love me wildly, you still won't listen when I ask you not to keep getting in touch with me. Hasn't it occurred to you that I'm trying to be by myself? And you've still got tomato sauce on the tip of your nose. Don't you have any tissues?')

'Psst,' says Martin in parentheses. 'There she is! Valerie Singleton. And she's with a chap!'

('No I haven't got any tissues. And even if I had it's no business of yours what there is on the end of my nose. I love you and I'll have tomato sauce on my nose if I so choose. Don't see why you agreed to come if you're going to argue the whole time.')

'She's shorter than I imagined. And where's the cat? You get used to the idea, don't you, of them having cats and the like. Remember Jason? Still, you never know with these TV people whether they're sincere on camera. She might hate cats. If you're looking for sincerity I don't think you need go any further than old Ted Moult. Even his name. I mean, if he hadn't been sincere, he wouldn't have been called Ted Moult. And you have the sweetest eyes I've ever seen.'

('I agreed to come because I was hoping to talk you out of this quest you seem to have regarding me. But I don't think it's going to work.'

The man, wearing a smile of resignation, plucks at her reappeared hand and looks at her forehead. 'So, you don't care about me then?'

'Oh there you go. Self self self. Anyway, that's not the point.'

'Of course it's the point. What's with this stuff where you actually keep away from the people you're close to?'

'It's all to do with finding yourself.'

'That's crap for a start. What does it mean? Finding yourself. And what're you going to do when you've found it? Give it away most likely to some bastard with a Ford Granada.'

'Who I give what away to is my affair.'

He kisses her hand. She reaches forward, examines him for a moment, then presses her mouth to his.)

'Don't be ridiculous,' says Mary. 'I haven't got sweet eyes or sweet anything else.'

Martin smiles. 'That's all right. I don't worry if I annoy you a little because I annoy most people when they're getting to know me. "Martin," they say, "you'd be a decent sort of chap if you could get to grips with how normal people behave." But who are these normal people? And what's so great about rushing around getting nowhere fast on the way to death? I can't cope with that. Just can't. And I've always been out on a limb. Then you came along and, well, something in me went twing.'

'Twing?'

'Yes, yes, absolutely. Twing. I loved you already. Always had. So I didn't see the need to work up to it. I can't handle people who leap about in discos or go boating on Sundays for months on end, playing a kind of game till they announce over moonlight and Martini that they love each other and there's supposed to be a difference from then on. And they tell all their friends and the friends join in with the celebrations, being thrilled and all that. Well, it seems a bit sick to me. Doesn't it to you? So I thought I'd come right out with it. Cut the middleman. We can go boating some other time. Oh look. Val's having Black Forest gâteau.'

(The kiss deepens, her hand cherishing his ear, his furrowing her hair. By mutual but unspoken agreement they stand, ready to leave. She picks up Proust, he *Marmosets*. Looking at one another, they head for the door. They'll be on a bed together, kissing each other's lips, hips, tips perhaps.)

Martin has a trace of saliva at the corner of his mouth. 'Yes, I can see this isn't making much sense to you and that's my fault. I didn't mean to overwhelm you. It's just that, well, don't you agree people should sort of take the bull by the horns? I reckon if people did it more – took bulls by horns – then we wouldn't be in such a twist. Yeah, that's it. Twist. We wouldn't be in one, though by "we" I don't mean you and me. But everyone generally. Do you know anyone who isn't in a twist? I don't.'

Mary's pushing back her chair, weaving through the tables to the courtyard and hiding behind a wall where she brings up her coffee, splash, like pouring it in reverse. (Matthew has already explained how he had to carry a suitable receptacle around with him for the first few weeks.) Slightly better then, she crosses the courtyard, slips through the gateway and slowly follows the steps to the road, where she pauses to catch her breath. Martin's on the far pavement, looking for her. She watches him pacing back and forth for a minute or two till he catches sight of her and beats his forehead with the base of his palm.

'I want to go home,' she calls.

She chooses the top deck of the yellow bus, sitting in the front seat, her hand attached to the chrome rail, Martin jigging beside her, rolling his ticket into a thin tube.

'I'm full of guilt now,' he's saying. 'I don't seem to have handled it too well back there. Sorry if I offended or disturbed you in some way. It truly wasn't my intention.'

Mary is still a little nauseous. 'Can't you stop keeping on just for a minute?'

He's laughing at himself, squinting through his rolled-up ticket. 'Yeah, I know I'm a bit over the top sometimes. It's usually because I'm nervous. And then there's an unfortunate aspect to my character which leads people to think I'm pretending. But I'd like to assure you that this is me. Really me. This is how I am.'

'Well, you have my deepest sympathy.'

'Sorry.' He's poking out his bottom jaw, exposing his teeth, groaning. Then his features relax. 'My mouth gets tense. This is an exercise I've developed to cure it. The idea is you make everything hurt, and you're so relieved when you stop doing it you end up relaxed. Do you get them? Tense mouths?'

The bus is stopping and starting through the thick of the city. Mary smokes prohibited cigarettes to calm down, nausea translating itself into the grins, oohs and ahs of these other travellers in their beige coats and sumptuous shoes. And through the window it seems people are exquisite, quite capable, hailing taxis, nodding with companions beneath toothpaste awnings or waiting for tomorrow in health-food doorways. The streets yawning, contracting, flowing freely or coming to a standstill with executives throwing their Sierras into short-cut cobbled side-roads, their suit jackets on hangers in the back, and there's a whole miasma of them beating through the city remote from the galaxy of her perceptions. And so is he, even, his head tight against the rattling window, clouding it with circles of breath; then he's leaning the other way, against her.

'We'll get you home. Never fear, Martin's here.'

Outside the sex shop someone in a chicken suit hops up and down beside a board advertising free-range eggs. Children are poking artificial feathers and giggling into their hands.

Martin makes the audible equivalent of the written sound *tsk*. 'Tsk,' he's saying. 'If you came home one day and told me you'd seen someone dressed as a chicken in the street, I wouldn't believe you. Modern life's like that, isn't it? The sort of thing people wouldn't believe in. Tsk.'

His hand falls over hers. She watches it carefully. 'Everything you say is so predictable.'

'I wouldn't have said so.'

'In fact you're a walking cliché.'

Leaning away from her a little, he looks into her eyes. 'And you're the best thing since sliced bread.'

A drawn-out silence in which Martin makes various attempts to untense his mouth, smacks his lips, shakes his head and *tsk*s. Mary has crossed her legs to muffle an aroma which has blossomed through her imagination, coming from there or from beneath her arms, yet the movement of the bus moistens the dream she often has for unhygienic coupling. *Come taste the irreligious bitters.* Martin is now twisting in his seat, slapping his knees.

'Funny, but I can remember it so clearly. It was the day in the market when there were rumours going round that Leslie Crowther had popped in. I hadn't been there long. I was waiting for customers but trying to look as if I wasn't waiting for them. Did you do that ? If they knew you were waiting for them it sort of drove them away. I didn't see Leslie but the chap on the fruit and veg stall – you know, the one in the blue coat and bottle-hat – said he got his autograph. And he was in hysterics because he reckoned he'd asked Leslie if he was going to write the autograph with a Crackerjack! pencil. Good old Leslie. *He's* cracked it. Anyway, I was standing by my table fiddling with a young cotoneaster and I saw you. Not that I hadn't seen you before, but I *saw* you and it was different this time. You were blowing your nose, if I recall. It was like I remembered you from somewhere. I loved you and *had* loved you. Something about you gave me courage and, I don't know, made me feel a long wait was over. Yeah, that was the feeling. A long wait was over. And you know those strange inward shivers people have? Well, I had one of those. And let me tell you, I haven't been able to shake it off. No. And I've tried, believe me. Spent days in my room doing just that – trying to shake it off. But the more I shook, the more it came to me: *I love her.* Don't laugh, but the feeling helped resolve a problem I've had for a long time. I felt, well, like a man. That's the daft part because you could look at me and say to yourself, "Well of course he's a man," but I've never known how my – if you like – Sebastian Flyte character could make headway in a world so heavily populated with Sylvester Stallones. I first spotted the problem at school when all the other kids were pretending to be Plastic Man. The thing was this. I never wanted to be Plastic Man. Course, you could easily assume there was some other hero I wanted to be, but that wasn't so. I didn't want to be anyone, not even Martin. And I couldn't believe in anything. The other kids would watch Batman and really get into it. But I was always put off, knowing he was just an average chap in silly clothes and that to one side of the Batcave there were men in polo-necks wielding cameras. I suppose you could say this disbelief was the flavour of my formative years. Then I saw you. And the only thing I wanted was to get to know you. And do you know what? Seeing you filled me with pride at being Martin; at having held on for so long.'

Sunlight slants across the city creating, at roof level, a clutter of triangular shadows and illuminating an alcove in the chapel frontage where three wooden peasants strike the hour against a brass bell with metal hammers. Beneath, on the pavement, solicitors in uniform stroll back and forth with red-ribboned packages, under their arms. The gaping streets are blue and unarguable. The bus rolls across plate-glass windows. Here and there strangers, through the dimples and swirls of bars, bistros, are chipping out conversations. Yes, down there a fair number of the population attach fingers to the stems of maroon wine-glasses and even from up here you can see the liquid's sparkle, hear it pumping through bottle-necks; cherry-red carpets, cherries on sticks, teeth through cocktail onions and the benevolent companionship instigated by those sweet little sip-things, their tingle tickle at the back of the throat. Naturally she'd like to be in those warm places with generous feelings because she suspects it's a farce to be this sick over nothing when everyone else... A farce. Can't even point to it and say, *There you are.* And she's tired of it and hasn't been sleeping properly despite the amount of sleep she's been having. Whoever heard of anything like that? Sleeping but not sleeping? Oh well, not properly. Because there's usually something niggling her dreams; an insect buzzing at the window or students next door thumping to enthusiastic lyrics. *The only way is UP, baby, for you and me now.*

'What happened then? Between you and your chap. Packed it in, did he?'

'Packed himself in.'

'And how would you feel, you know, if he walked back through the door tomorrow?'

She rubs her nose. 'Fucking horrified.'

(Hmmm. An expletive. From a *woman*. And such cherry lips.)

She's remembering Paul eating her, that is French and everything, his moist body sprawled between her legs, his fingers pulling her thighs apart the better to get at you, my dear, but then he raised his chin and retched. She slithered backwards in response but the retch ended in wind because there was nothing in him to come up. After a decent interval and a sort of apology he dragged her back, opened her up and continued. He loved to suckle her till she grew mushy, her arms thrown back in surrender. A few days later he was at the party, and the next morning Billy the Boot came round to break the news and maybe have sex with her again, well, hadn't she ached for it last time? Only have to look at her and she wets up. 'The pigs were there,' said Billy the Boot. He'd got pissed off with being interrogated. And now he took hold of Mary's shoulders, pushed her into a corner, unhooked her belt and with one hand was trying to pull her jeans down but she'd had enough and smacked her fist against the side of his head, making him hop round for a while. Then, swearing revenge, he left. She slithered down the angle of the wall, curled up on the floor-cushion and held a private wake for the absent dead, waving neatly to the raincoated China girl who was on her way to work.

6

S HE'S THINKING of a time when she'd been crying for
hours and her mother wanted to know exactly what the
matter was. Exactly. The sky had been hanging in the trees
all day. Then, an indeterminate time later, she was walking over
green and white tiles towards a small door with a reinforced
window, the dark nurse beside her saying, 'Don't worry, it's just
an observation room.' And the first time she saw Paul (an image
tucked in between heaving over porridge) must have been days
afterwards when, having come round a bit more, she was once
again allowed to sit with the others in the day-room. Her seat
was made of a midnight-blue rexine material which stuck to her
as she dampened. And she was being encouraged by one or two of
the patients to join in choruses of 'Old Macdonald' with a trio of
domestics who were polishing the floor, cleaning the windows,
dashing away with the smoothing irons. (The monk playing
table-tennis sang, 'And on that farm he had some Diazepam, ee-
i-ee-i-o.') Paul was the one at the telescopic end of the ward
gazing at squirrels through the large window. It was a place for
loopies and Mary was shaking in her hospital dressing-gown and
slippers as the others sang, looked at the underwear pictures in
Vogue, trailed fingers along the prefabricated bookcase full of
unread paperbacks, fought the cheeseplant or held one-sided
conversations with the Blob in the chair next to theirs. And the

Blobbiest of them, she later learned, was called Matilda. The poor soul had come on to this acute ward for a few days due to a lack of space elsewhere. Matilda's day consisted of becoming more comfortably draped in the wheeled apparatus she would have called home if she could have spoken. *Under the shade of a coolabah tree.* The monk was hopping back and forth at this end of the table-tennis table, his brown habit and open-toed sandals hopping with him, and the first words she heard him speak rather than sing were, 'Oh fuck it!' when his return ball to the one-legged sailor lodged in the limp green net. *With a cluck-cluck here and a cluck-cluck there.* Nurses, some pink, some purple, one blue, wandered through the day-room periodically, cracking therapeutic witticisms, playfully chastising the monk for his language, wiping saliva, of which there was gallons, from Matilda's chin and making sure her brake was on. And in case she hanged herself in those early days, Mary was accompanied by the dark nurse whenever she wanted to use the toilet.

('Oh look,' says Martin, 'a Renault Dauphine. Haven't seen one of those for...'

The nurse was polishing her fingernails while Mary, drawers at her knees and not nice drawers either, pissed into the bowl and there was such a powerful tang to it the nurse said, 'Well my darlin', you could put some ice and lemon in a glass of *that* and have a pretty good evenin'.' A mixed ward. Mad with mad together in the day-room but segregated at night lest one should couple with another to produce permanently chuckled offspring. Her mother was bringing in grapes and knickers and the general opinion went round that it was sad such gentleness in a girl could lead to these misfortunes. So she waited in her chair for several more days till Paul and Thomas the monk introduced themselves and the future began. As soon as she was allowed to wear her ordinary clothes, her two friends frequently took her to the tea-bar-stroke-social-club where longstays ate nuts and nuts ate biscuits and scarlet-nosed aesthetes argued with the universe in corners. The hospital in a green-and-white-tiled world of its own, its secrets and charms unveiled by Thomas, who one day led her along side-corridors full of dusk to a dark store-cupboard whose doors he threw open to reveal a cubic space stacked with tins of Italian plum tomatoes

She's pressing the bell for the bus to pull in at her stop; Martin is yawning then following her down the steps on to the street; Mary, standing with him by the converted church, saying, 'I suppose you ought to come back for a coffee.' Martin arranges himself before whispering, 'Oh well, just for a minute then.' A wooden hoarding neatly fixed between the twin spires of the church reads: TYRE PRICES SLASHED, and two men in the car park beneath the spires climb into a Beetle and drive away, loud music through their open windows: *You gotta fast car, I gotta ticket to anywhere*. Martin's wallowing in one of his finest days, having witnessed the conception and pregnancy of a dream and now awaiting its birth. Yes, give him a cup of coffee then send him on his way. By then a nap will be justified, surely. After all, a sleep is just a sleep; it doesn't have to be a symptom of wanting to escape or anything. Just nature's way of saying for Christ's sake lie down. That's all. Then tackle a few chores. Mary in cotton scarf and pinny brandishing dustpan and brush. The thought of it. *You may say I'm a dreamer, but I'm not the only one*. The street busy with maidens in black stockings, gentlemen pretending to be retired sea captains from an unfought war, the pavement softened for her like walking a trampoline till she reaches her door, twists the key and pushes it open with her foot. The hall swings into view. Twisting herself, she sees the figure in the chandelier room shaking its head. Martin has obviously been preparing for the mess that will greet him in the hope of taking things in his stride. *Fallen Women and What to Do*. Through the gloom into a dank living room, empty of anything Habitat would recommend. It's like an abandoned charity shop, and Mary pulls off her anorak and goes into the kitchen while Martin reviews the scenes of her crime. Plenty of cobwebs, yes, but she'll proclaim herself to be protective of innocent spiders. Stained sofa. Compacted rugs. 'Ah this must be the fellow,' he'll whisper to himself picking up the photo of Paul. There's the enemy. Though who can blame him for fleeing from this? She needs rescuing, that's for sure. He'll be spotting the pair of knickers under the chair, burn marks on top of the cupboard and, in one corner, the pieces of a broken serving dish.

Billy the Boot did it in the kitchen with a length of lead piping.

Waiting for the kettle, Mary steps outside. The woman in the sky is standing by the table, looking out but not seeing, hands linked loosely in front of her while a man (not the man who's usually there) creeps up to her and wraps his arms round her breasts. And though at first she attempts to heave his arms away, her legs soon yield and she's risking his cheek with the backs of her fingers. They remain just so for a minute or more, becoming one figure, a statuette of infidelity. Then, breaking away, the man moves round to face her while the woman looks at the floor. He's twisting his head from side to side, then throwing out his arms and waggling his hands.

Mary makes the coffee and takes it to Martin who's examining the sole of his shoe. She's staring through the window into this irregular road, idylls of the countryside continuing their spells of retrospect. And the sadness of any moment is that you're in it with your gut-ache, migraine, sore feet. She turns to look at

Martin just as Martin turns to look at her. He's resting his coffee on the arm of the chair and shaking his head.

'Right then. So this is where you live, eh?'

She turns back. Still, he's not bad-looking and there are moments when his naïveté has its charms, and whatever else you may say about him he's sincere. But at the same time there's probably a lie infecting his sincerity. She's in two minds, each spying on the other and down below (batten the hatches) the creature's growing damper still and twists of mushroom rise like the animated flavours of Bisto. Living's curtains. A window-pane divided into four. Strangers strolling from one honeysuckled edge to another, the figure in the window opposite standing sideways, gazing at a photo-frame.

'Yeah, I'm sorry if I've gone, well, quiet, but I'm happy, do you understand? Rather happy and that's that. Happy to be with you. Happy to sit in your chair. Happy to ... to love you and everything.'

'Amen.'

'Exactly.'

'Who am I to condemn ecstasy?'

'Quite. Sorry. Didn't mean...'

It was a moonstruck night of screech-owls, platinum shadows, the sprinkled perfume of Queen Anne lace and grass cold underfoot; and as she walked she was undoing her clothes, unveiling a silver skin to nibbles of wind, her undergarments last of all, naturally, watching them billow through a night sky till she reached the fringe of willow and tiptoed to the stream's edge, drawing breath as she stepped in and the water tightened round her shins. She could make out the shape of a cow rubbing itself against railings on the opposite bank and she was managing to whisper, 'Love you, Satan,' though with little conviction. It was more the simplicity of moonlight and a need to be taken, somehow. She waded in till pebbles in shallower parts gave way to sand or mud which sucked her foot and the water crept to her thighs, rippling against *this*. And if Satan had come galloping she would have abandoned herself to his instruction. All this speculation over the gender of God but none about Satan. He's a *he* all right. The freedoms of his promise. A chill outside instigating warmths within till she was liquid and, reaching forward, sank beneath the surface before throwing herself up in an ecstasy of cold. He'd wait at the edge of the stream, scraping his hoof, miraculously erect and without morality. *Save these interludes up for Martin.* She was brushing the water from her hair wading against a silver current, the blood running to the most succulent quarters bringing them a tumescence, a pride, her arms thrown back to exaggerate them. By this time she knew the stream well – its whispers, its creatures rustling on the dark bank, the dangers of the moon – and as soon as she was in the correct position she took hold of the willow root, followed it down to the submerged knot and ground herself against it whispering, 'Come to me, Satan' till she came and sank, exhausted. Then, wading back to the bank, she pulled her empty bottle from the undergrowth (placing it just so); splashed back into the stream for handfuls of mud and lay open to the moon on the moist grass, smearing her breasts and legs as a sweet unguent for the rhythms of the bottle, a charming little game to play in the mongrels of the night.

'Look,' says Martin quietly. 'Your drink was getting cold so I took the liberty of making you another. I hope you don't mind.'

'No. That's fine. Thank you. Just leave it on the chair.'

'You've beautiful skin.'

'Yes. It goes right round.'

'And it was two sugars, wasn't it? You see, to my way of

thinking there are two types: mottled is one; fine-grained another. Yours is fine-grained. Not a trace of mottle.'

'Yes, that's right. Two sugars.'

Through the window she sees a line of blue-grey walls, orange roofs, pavements uneven with the scars of a long-gone avenue of trees and, in a square of soil by the elderly figure's front door, another smudge of cotoneaster. It grows everywhere yet hardly anyone mentions it. A shrub planted not for its own sake, she supposes, but to conceal bare patches or ugly bits of workmanship. And here's Martin in the background, sipping coffee, forgiving her this lifestyle, her secrets, in advance, his infatuation for a painted doll like the Russian kind you unscrew and there's another just the same only smaller, and this familiar dream rearing between her thighs which she could unzip for him for a laugh, ha-ha, though Paul's the lucky one. When she really thinks about it moods are like liquid, beautiful liquid, running from a soaked brush down a sheet of paper and once she dreamed (when her Dylan days were perfect and she was easy as the willow boughs) of being a Parisian on an old bench in a white square of pigeons and cafés, a fiddle player in the distance wearing a hooped shirt, and she'd have been passing the time of day with Manet beneath wonderful umbrellas. *Kisses for me, save all your kisses for me.* Let's go nice and mad. And Matthew's voice repeating the phrase 'Give up then give in, give up then give in.' That was the day he took her to look at the hospital as part of what he called her 'fresh perspective'. They were sitting on the wall in the car park gazing at mellow lawns, fir trees, the crazy magnitudes of red brick. Then they travelled back to the city on a yellow bus, Matthew twiddling his fingers and humming his favourite sobriety tunes while Mary wondered if she might throw open the emergency doors and jump out to avoid dealing with things. But that was then and now is now. Martin is reviewing the vision he had of her by the cotoneaster that day and now realising it was just a *hint* of what entertainments were to come. He's turning to look at her. She can make out the shallows of his reflection as she refocuses on the surface of the window. *Yes, well, sorry, but here she is and it's all there by golly; all there, in the way she's standing, sunlight enrapturing her hair, those dainty fingers twiddling on the window-sill and her shoes, the left one resting on its scuffed tip. There's a symphony emanating from her, harmonising with his. And he'd do anything she asked, anything: handstands, solo pogo-sticking expeditions, bear hunting on the Waltons' mountain with Jimbob. He's prepared to be a fool if necessary; needs nothing more than this tolerance of his devotion. Loves her to bits.* She can feel it, beating at the back of her neck as, outside, women come and go talking of setting lotion, salmonella, Imran Khan (the most perfect delivery in cricket). But that's it. She'll turn around in rhapsody, sit, become reason itself yet she's numb with quartered window-pane and a cacophony of song as she pulls her finger across the glass, its tip turning yellow, dark yellow. And she's realising that the term 'dark yellow' is never used. Nicotine. And now with a strip of grime removed, the road becomes more brilliant still, the elderly figure opposite settling into a fireside chair and she's left with just the top of its silvered coiffure in a room of white walls, plaster mouldings and the blue chandelier. At intervals pages of a newspaper appear at one side of the chair to be shaken and reorganised. *The Times* no doubt.

'If you aren't careful, Mary, this one will get cold too. In my experience there's nothing quite so uninviting as a cold coffee.'

'I'll be there in two shakes of a lamb's tail.'

'Hey. Funny you saying that. My Aunt Gertrude used to say it all the time.'

She's figuring she'll end up having to invent a life rather than falling in with conviction to what many refer to as 'the swing of things'. Otherwise she'll be consigned to watch the comings and goings of terminal persons in city windows or the racing of panic-attackers for the morning paper to see what horrors have taken place. 'Bush in Sanity Probe'. There are usually children with no legs in flea-bitten hospitals or seagulls flapping mournfully in oil to ruin one's capacity for the romantic, though Martin has managed to remain unscathed, popping up from behind a shrub to scratch for happiness in the most unlikely terrain. She's the one for him, by the looks of it. His Cleopatra. So he can bear this interminable sipping of coffee, the examination of his shoes and the lines on his palms with frequent glances at the sweeps of her shoulder, the succulence of buttock in those remarkable jeans. She can't have had a new pair since God knows when. Maybe scruffiness ensues when you've been crazy, haute-coiffure falling off a list of priorities along with bathroom cabinets, Burgundy suite-covers, perusal of the FT index. And now, a finger between her legs to scratch another itch, she's pulling herself from the window and sinking into her chair, then smiling at Martin in compensation for her general silence. He pulls himself upright.

'It's good sitting here with you. It feels natural, if you know what I mean.'

She nods. Takes a sip. Picks at a thread on her jeans.

'Yes. Old Aunt Gertrude. She had a bad time once. A bit like you. She used to be, oh, fabulously rich. Married to a distant relation of President Mitterrand. Anyway, after he died – her husband, that is – she went to, well, pieces. (Not that you're as bad as that.) It turned out she had one of those brain diseases. You know: the ones that are always named after Austrians. One minute she was grieving like anyone else, the next she was wandering the streets half naked. Time after time the police would ring my mother and say Aunt Gertrude was at the station. This carried on for ages. Then she was run over.'

Mary spits coffee back into her cup. Martin laughs too.

And it was a ridiculous thing, looking back – stealing Matilda from her corner of the ward, finding a spare wheelchair for Mary to ride in then Paul and Thomas pushing them along the green and white corridors singing *Oh the grand old Duke of York,* Matilda in paroxysms of *something,* through double-door after double-door to the farthest regions of the mad, some of whom were pacing up and down wearing hospital suits, busy fingers playing behind humped backs (the smell of urine superseding Harpic). From one ward, she heard strains of Tony Bennett and other cool American melodies. The old men and women were pacing to a white line drawn across the corridor, then instinctively turning round to pace back, chewing continually. And the corridor linked each and every ward in a circle probably a quarter of a mile long, a journey in which the three companions and Matilda glimpsed all conditions from post-natal depressives to pre-war orphans, whose wards may have been an imaginary manor house and the other patients their servants. In the longest stretch of downward-sloping corridor a race was undertaken in which Thomas caused Matilda's feet to knock over a cheeseplant and the walls rang to a mixture of his laughter and her equivalent of it, which involved the expulsion of much saliva. Thomas had tissues to wipe it away from her maroon dress. This place where the unthinkable was commonplace and which for a time Mary became quite fond of, once the heeby-jeebies had died down, those rubber wheels squealing over tiles, Thomas's face red as boyhood, longstays visible through the windows trowelling among tea roses and honeysuckles, caps askew and knees worn from prayers to an ebullient god, and she was noticing Paul's eyes, their rage and bitterness shackled by tablets, and the meltdown of limbs beneath Thomas's habit. Soon Matilda's brittle legs came into contact with the shins of a nursing officer whistling out of a ward and the group was warned to slow down and consider other patients, most of whom he believed wouldn't take kindly to racket on Wednesday afternoons, and Matilda, so it seemed, was a length of gristle pushed to one side of a fat man's dinner plate yet happy to be so as they moved on, Thomas reaching down at intervals to haul her to the back of her apparatus, Paul pushing Mary's chair with confidence and Mary wallowing back, a cigarette between her lips. Near Ward Four, Thomas nodded reverentially to a patient being wheeled from the Electro-Convulsive Therapy Suite whose grin, he conjectured, was now that of a middle-American testament lover.

'That electricity kicks the shit out of you,' he was saying.

Martin, having recently finish yawning, leans towards her.

'Penny for them.'

'Just thinking.'

'Ah. Thinking.'

Thinking she ought to review and prevent this China girl thing. After all, she has been tumbling to the eiderdown of Mary's imagination for, oh, decades, China girl, an emerald in her fingers, the room immaculate with spring, yellow flowers in crystal vases, birdsong through an open window, the crack and flap of brilliant curtains, China girl's hair drifting across a cream pillowcase and beams of sunlight springing from a stained-glass mobile.

'This is a beautiful stone,' China girl always says. She's tentatively wrapped in a silken dressing-gown and as she raises her knee the gown sighs either side of her leg.

Mary waits innocently on a nearby chair, a tumbler in her hands. 'Yes, beautiful,' she's saying, the sway of China girl's white thigh somehow crucifying the room.

A polite cough as Martin assumes an air of sagacity.

'Yes, I've a lot to thank you for, really. I've even joined a library. Since all this began, you know, I've wanted to explore the world in whatever way I can, and reading seems to be one of the best, don't you agree? I'll let you into a little secret. The last book I'd read till recently was *Five Go to Kirrin Island*. But knowing you has given me a whole new lease on life. Since last week I've finished one and started another so I'm actually really pleased with myself. Mind you, I made a bit of a mistake with the first, some hocus-pocus about witchcraft in the medical profession – *The Satanic Nurses*. Didn't enjoy it a bit but I said to myself, "Martin, it's no good reading if you're not going to stick each book out to the end, otherwise how are you going to develop a broad perspective?" Since then I've started another called *Titus Groan*, which is altogether better. In fact I'd say it's a mighty work. Mighty. I'm on about page twelve and there's this chap, see, and he's in a room full of wooden carvings that other chaps have ... well, carved. There's this really weird castle and the carving chaps live outside the...'

'Please don't tell me.'

'I'm really really enjoying it. Funny, because I'd spotted it before, but I've always been put off by the front cover. You must have seen it. Not exactly bedtime reading but then I suppose it's what people call Literature rather than just a book.' He clicks his tongue against the roof of his mouth then forms a wise triangle with his arms as a balance for his chin. 'Yes, I want to read everything now because, well, because of you. And do you know something? You're absolutely...'

'Please, don't. Just...'

'You're going to hate me for saying this, but I've a strong feeling that a good chinwag would help snap you out of yourself. Not that it's bad to be *in* yourself. It's just that, well...'

Reading. Another of Matthew's suggestions as he led her, his arms illustrating the world, along a darkened street. Mary bunched up beside him, and there were walls of moist glistening blue and, behind the kebab house, a platoon of dustbins one of which was a third full of old food. Matthew called these expeditions the 'flesh of living', the putrefying carcass of the whole damn thing. Spotting flashes of panic in her eyes, he laid a palm on her shoulder and gently eased her forward.

'It's necessary to find a balance,' he was saying, 'a balance between fighting your condition and not fighting your condition. Courage and acceptance.'

She had no idea whether to lie down and drown or stand up, fists raised, prepared to give an uppercut to the worst of it. She remembers the unconditional cold of the street, the ease of Matthew's footsteps, his unmitigated cheerfulness and, as they reached the top of the hill, the spread of white and yellow city lights and lemon moon above.

'I don't really want a chinwag. I'm not up to them. I haven't read the book you're talking about and I probably...'

'Oh, please don't think I was suggesting...'

'I wasn't. I'm just not...'

'Oh.' He's rearranging himself in his chair. 'I was talking to a chap about books at the market. You know, the one with the paperback stall. And he was saying the only way to sort out whether a book's Literature or not is to imagine the author in the bathroom. If you can't picture him or her sitting on the toilet then the book's most probably Literature. Thinking about it afterwards, I could see he was right in a way. I mean it's hard to visualise Mervyn Peake going, but Barbara Cartland's a cinch.'

He smiles in anticipation of Mary smiling, but she's busy with her coffee. The room darkens slightly.

'Yes. Gorgeous. That's what I was going to say a moment ago.

You're gorgeous. I know nobody uses that word any more, but it's the one I'd go for, and I think it's important someone should tell you. And nothing's going to make me change my mind.'

He's sweeping his hand in an arc to indicate the nothings which won't be influencing him: the room, the earth, Mary's hair. Who cares? She nods. And yes, she's been using the image of China girl to reactivate a grey heart. The very thing Matthew would call 'diluting her inadequacies'. He's been saying that her brain will be subject to such fantasies for some time to come; it's its way of compensating, so she shouldn't take much notice of them. And it would be foolish to underestimate the damage she's inflicted on the old cerebellum. Then, unexpectedly, this moment of time is a prism, sunlight fragmented into colours over a piece of paper and China girl's the human symbol of it, her fine slim leg poking through the silken dressing-gown, a soft white thigh, the emerald held aloft and Mary making dream progress to the bedside. Then an amber night, China girl's smile the most haunting, the most romantically provocative, the knot of that same dressing-gown unfurling by degrees; a patch of abdomen moving as she breathes; the slightest suggestion of breast. Though what's the point in dreaming it? Mary sinking on to the bedclothes, China girl's mouth opening, the unsteady reflections of candle flame in her eyes and, at the far end of brief conversations, a small hand resting in the dip of Mary's waist.

She remembers walking with Peter one afternoon along a water-logged track, an early winter sunlight yellowing the trees, the low banks swamped by the reds and golds of fallen leaves and, further along, the high, scrub-covered hillside with outcrops of limestone they later climbed. Towards the top, laughing with breathlessness they tucked into a hollow for cigarettes, a fragrant wind brushing Peter's hair. Oh yes, she was cold and Peter offered her the T-shirt he was wearing beneath his jumper and had to half-strip to get it off. She was pulling off her own jumper to put it on and loved Peter's white chest and the faint undulations of muscle at his stomach. He'd brought a pad and pencil along, hoping to capture moments of the afternoon, all love for her and the brilliance of her smile as his lips squeezed tighter still. And in his eyes the glint of brief wisdoms and the pleasure of listening to crows arguing in grey boughs. But then she was catching sight of his skew-whiff head and the stray lump of limestone between them in the hollow, and imaginary hands were reaching for the stone and striking him repeatedly till his skull collapsed. This imagination followed her all afternoon along the ridge of the hill, over drystone walls and round the ancient tumulus just as, when she was younger, songs used to play over and over without end.

Martin's digging his little finger into the corner of his left eye. 'This could be the wrong moment to ask, but I was wondering what the prospects were of, you know, seeing you again. I mean, I desperately want to. Of course I realise that might not apply to you. Strange world, isn't it, with all these difficulties? If we do see each other, I obviously want you to be happy with the idea. If you're not, then although I'd still want to see you again I'm sort of prepared not to, providing it makes you happy though it wouldn't, well, make me happy. I mean, it would be a bit like cooking a meal and … not eating it.' He lifts his knees, lowers them. 'And then there's intuition which tells me not only that we'll carry on seeing each other but that we *ought* to. I feel I must have faith in my original vision at the market.'

Ah. The Cotoneaster Factor. She'd forgotten that. She supposes he's not so much falling in love with her as picking his way down a rockface towards it; the most difficult attempt he's ever made and his thrill's the greater in those circumstances. Some women, why, they're just hip-hops down the gentlest of meadow slopes with eternity as the reward, but perhaps he's come to appreciate footholds and fingertips and the joys of being ropeless.

She's lighting a cigarette, determined to tell a little of her history while leaving out some of the more liquid aspects. 'Martin, there are one or two things I should tell you.'

He's peering at her, an empathetic smile on his lips. 'Oh, right. You fire away then.'

As she completes her edited recitation he's stroking his forehead with the back of his hand and on the full stop of her last words (bottle neck) he stands, yawns, ambles to the window (hands in pockets), looks left and right, comes back to the sofa, raises his cup and eyebrows by way of asking if he can have another coffee, then, at her nod, escapes into the kitchen humming 'Jake the Peg'. A few minutes later he returns, his coffee black this time because the milk has run out. Once more he chooses to stand at the window, sipping towards the elderly figure who's performing an arm and hip exercise to unheard music. Martin's breath brushes steam from his coffee against the window-pane. In a moment or so he resumes his hum and sits down again, resting the cup carefully on the floor beside him before cracking individual finger joints, throwing back his head and sighing at the ceiling.

'Yes, well, I suppose we all have a few skeletons in our cupboards. Things we'd rather weren't true. I did some awful things with a sherbet dab once.'

Mary puffs out her cheeks, blowing in disbelief. 'What's the matter with you? Why do you put up with everything I say and do?'

'Well,' he says, turning his attention to fingernails and the moons thereof. 'I've been thinking about that and I've decided it's because I love you. Yes, that's what it is.'

'And hasn't any of it bothered you?'

'Oh well, bits here and there like the stream and what have you, but then I thought, "Ah, what the hell, Martin, doesn't everyone?" Oh, maybe not in the dark and maybe not with mud and a bottle but, then, they're only symbols after all. I mean, take a trip downtown and you'll see shops selling, you know, vibrators and stuff in the shape of … them. How's that any different, when you boil it down? I remember I started thinking about, well, *it* at eight.'

And he was still thinking about it at half-past nine.

'Of course, when you're eight you're not quite sure what it is you want to do even though you desperately want to do it. But if you want my opinion, I reckon we should get the whole thing out into the open. I often think about people like the Pope. I mean, he's bound to have his difficult moments, isn't he? And if only people like him would get it out into the open, just think how relieved everyone would be. Keeping desires secret because we think of them as, well, sinful is what makes them sinful. No, I don't mind what you've said. Just shows you're human and I'll love you till…'

Matthew has said she should write everything down. Everything. Believes she should meet the future clean, an open book. Darknesses cherished could re-infect her spirit. But she's wondering how far that goes. Who decides what a darkness is and what it isn't? He had an answer, naturally: 'Whatever disturbs your memory of your present living – that's a darkness.' No other guideline was necessary. Regret nothing and there's nothing to regret; the spirit, he's sure, has a natural mechanism for illuminating these fundamental perspectives. Meanwhile, she's at the mirror, watching as Martin watches her. This puffed face and these jaundiced eyes may not belong to her any more. Sensing a moment of crisis, Martin comes to her, rests his hand on her shoulder, squeezes through to the bone, then returns to the sofa where he adopts a regal posture, a knee on each hand and a look of 'So what?' round his cheeks and shoulders. His touch lingers as sweat trickles from the hair in her underarms and seeps through the soft skin at the far reaches of her abdomen. Though he must have taken deep breaths of her, he doesn't seem to mind and now chews his bottom lip, wondering perhaps where to drag the conversation. She's remembering the glitter of sycamores, footfalls through avenues of purple rhododendron, echoes of laughter from ramblers high above, the path she followed winding downwards to a cottage made of gingerbread, perhaps, a German shepherd dog snarling through its white-painted fence. Then a tunnel, moist and red-bricked leading to crooked steps and the thick shade of a cedar tree softening unreadable headstones.

But in this room there's only rebellion of the liver and the misted image of Martin as she winks at him in the mirror and, jerking his chin, he winks back.

7

A POINT HIGH above the city, binoculars following a horizon of tightly terraced hills, patches of woodland, church spires, a pair of cooling towers each with its rain cloud; over this way, slate roofs, geometric roads, flamingo streelights and, in the midst of them, an undulating park with a large pond, tethered boats, swans, a bandstand; over there the river, skeletons of bulrushes at its fringe, January strollers along a tree-lined promenade and, in summer, there will be bags of crumbs for ducks, silken willows, lovers trailing fingers through weed-green water. The castle beyond is an undecorated cake rising above tight Near Eastern streets and the grey uniformity of the motorway. And just down there, tucking towards the foot of this hill, are silver windows, a yellow-painted pub, packed car parks and the skyward architecture of administrative buildings. Look at this broad heart which won't stop beating, streams of the anonymous through arterial streets, each cell with an idea, a memory, a plan, a bag or hat. Beyond the butter-coloured hospital is a confusion of steeper, more ancient streets where second-hand shops squeeze one against the other, the most squalid of them managed by a blasphemous Scottish woman in trews and dimpled spectacles selling cooker pieces, umbrella frames, plastic macintoshes, spineless annuals commemorating the Coronation. It would be impossible to pick out Mary's location from here since she's so small in the grand similarity,

86

but in a general sense she's over there, down a side-road among a
score of other side-roads. It's hard to have faith in her need to
exist as an individual. Any problems she may have had are
quickly suffocated by the grandeur of the larger body. A city,
after all, is just the sum of its acceptable parts. And a stone's
throw from the tips of these shoes is the razzmatazz of Gossamer
Street, its scatter of individuals wandering this way, that, laden,
unladen, happy, unhappy or, best of all, happy *and* unhappy. On
foot, men are coming and going with women, women with men.
Most of the time one suspects they have a lighter, more satisfying
life than one's own, talking as they wander of extraordinary
somethings, pausing to admire wooden toadstools in fashionable
gift-shop windows. Almost everything's available in Gossamer
Street: faded jeans with pre-frayed holes, tubes of oil paint all
colours of the world, reproduction reproduction furniture, poly-
thene Gorbachevs, ham and anchovy pizzas, imitation water-
falls, fluorescent yo-yos. Occasionally the men and women pass a
person with olive skin in the doorway of an unfrequented
restaurant, where straw hats, green bottles and plastic lobsters
hang in a tangle of nets across the window. And further down, in
a bookshop just for Christians (among leaflets to be filled in if you
wish to go walking with God in Crickhowell for the weekend) lie
numerous copies of *How to Cope* by Patience Strong. Next door is
a holiday shop, its display a magnificent Boeing 747 dangling on
strings. Passing by, a lollipop lady, a tramp, a mayoress, a
student, a waitress, an uncommitted gangster with concealed
water-pistol, a forgotten rock-star carrying a bag of peanut-
butter-and-cocaine sandwiches and, last of all, a China girl so
beautiful that men in general won't look at her, though one
drinking an Old Sumatran in the overhead café peers down with
much agitation of his teaspoon.

*   *   *

Mary had been trying to arrange her bedroom in the city house as the old one had been, but it looked uncomfortable, awkward, and those other buildings cast shadows against her window. Often she caught the local train to nowhere in particular and was carried through emerald ravines and wet tunnels hewn from rock and past pale cliffs to the river which was warm with butter parasols, melted swans, couples blending into courtship among restless willows. The train would proceed along its silver rails through fields of oak and thickets of blackberry to a separate landscape of tubular factories black with waste and trails of saffron smoke, though once it had been marshland and the Regency farmhouses were still stranded there among greywater ditches and soot-coloured trees. At the terminus she'd wait on the platform, watching waterbirds as they pecked over blue mud or listening to the conversations of old railmen through the office window. Catching a return train she'd go beyond her stop, past melancholy back gardens, light blue gas-holders, rows of allotments, asphalt playgrounds, then scrapyards, half a dozen of them, the claws of cranes swinging wrecks into tidy rows. There were dandelion sidings with aerosol *Hellos*, then shunting yards where men in yellow jackets ate sandwiches from grey shoulderpacks; on, on, to the mainline station, a perfect place to grow sad about yourself on black platforms while strings of carriages were being pulled from under the scooped roof into the sun or, with a smell of diesel and newsprint, into this dimness further dimmed by the glare of billboards advertising yellow beefburgers, unreadable books, mood-altering cans of this and that. She'd come across men with bags gazing at train-time monitors who'd then make seats out of that same baggage. Wouldn't sit with anyone. Or young women scuffing shoes at the far end of the platform as porters drove strings of luggage trolleys through brown double-doors. Other people had come to see other people off, a kiss through the window, 'Don't forget to write, give my

love to Florrie, thank you for the lovely bracelet, I'll treasure it.'
Then flats of hands stroking goodbye as the train wove out.
Maybe the man beneath the station clock was having a meno-
pause, hoping things would be different if 'Shy and lonesome
(but good with dogs) of Peckham' showed up. Though Mary
tried on several occasions, she couldn't run because places were
all the same if you took yourself along too fast. So she walked
back under rumbling flyovers, through green underpasses and
broad top-hat streets with tinted windows, the old buildings
being restored, roads heavy with yellow buses and, at the
kerbside, she'd see pink women whose leather bags were decor-
ated with blue and grey diamonds. And it was some boast of the
city that in its central area you need hardly cross a road, but the
boast was more of a rationalisation of the truth that cars enjoyed
the sunlight while walkers tunnelled and rose, pausing at the top
of the steps to re-instruct their sense of direction. Some underpasses were softened with Grecian seascapes you'd never reach,
while others chinkled to the tills of small shops too stuffy to
linger in, then coffee parlours where veal-skinned nobodies
stared at inebriates, flute-players, off-duty decapitators or fat
tramps in spittle-black with yawning tales of a desert campaign.
Then she'd come up into oblongs of brilliance, a concrete
toytown littered with designer drinking places of navy dark
furniture, padded bars, microwave pies. At the busiest intersec-
tion, still free of an underpass, traffic drew to a halt while posses
of strangers responded to green flashes and cantered to a cobbled
island, where they waited a second time. Beyond them stood the
award-winning rhomboid police headquarters and the hush of a
sand-yellow magistrate's court both built above drug-smuggling
bierkellers. She walked. Streets made vivid, swift; strangers were
a flourish of good humour and pastel against Louisiana shop-
fronts. Cafés, too, from the dried-tomato-sauce cholesterol kind

to those redolent of Jean-Paul Sartre, with coloured umbrellas, boulevards and young women piercing their palms with knives in the name of something complicated. Mary carried a book in her pocket: *The Wednesday Carousel*. Beautiful book with an illustration on the cover of a woman with fair hair and black clothing sitting on a children's roundabout in the dark, gazing out of the cover at whoever might care. Soon, whatever café Mary had found would swing, extend, fill the street, and living was a nosegay all right, a posy, a place to slink, celebrate. She wanted to be the woman on the roundabout for a while but then she realised that to achieve ambitions of this kind you had to be oblivious to anyone envying you and, above all, you had to be alone as you twisted through the dark.

Beginning with a moment of consciousness like a seed, the room grows, fattens, bursts into pale bloom. Mary is the stamen at its centre, her perfumes the petals around which Martin is buzzing first this way then that.

'And let me see,' he's saying, before *The Satanic Nurses* I was reading the autobiography of a Russian philosopher. Dimitri Slinkov. Yes, that's the name.'

Mary rests her head against the mirror. She's breathing deeply. Puffs of mushroom have risen from the deepness of her. Martin's waiting to see if she'll reply, but she allows her silence to speak for itself.

'I'd never heard of him before, but I reckon he's one of these people everyone ought to know about. Yes, Russian. Died in about, oh, 1930. I was browsing in the library – you know how you do – and the reason I picked the book up in the first place was because it was under G instead of S. People just put them back willy-nilly, don't they? Anyway, the flyleaf was raving about him, so I took it out.'

(That is, mushrooms prior to cooking, recently plucked from the woodland floor and popped into your basket.)

Squinting, Martin pulls his finger along the base of his eye-socket as if beginning a process by which he'll eventually erase himself.

'There was a whole lot in the book about his life and everything, but it was what he *thought* that was important. I don't want to go into it too deeply but from what I could gather he based much of his philosophy on the idea that disadvantages were actually advantages. That was the gist of it, anyway.'

Mary's rocking from side to side in front of the mirror, hoping that her reflection will snag on something out of frame and not reappear.

'Is that it?'

Martin sniffs. 'No, of course not. There were over four hundred pages of detailed stuff about his philosophy, his friend-ships, his attitude to his violent mother and his love for his wife who was for a long while his greatest influence but who ran off with a peasant.'

'And did he see that as an advantage?'

'Well, I can't remember whether it happened before or after he developed the idea.'

Mary is now rocking back and forth, catching the mantelpiece each time she's in danger of tipping.

'And if he saw disadvantages as advantages, does that mean he saw advantages as disadvantages? I mean, if he did, there was a risk of him going round in circles, wasn't there?'

'Probably. Look, do we have to go on with this? I was a bit stupid to mention it. I've just realised that if some Russian came up to you and said your present disadvantage was in fact an advantage you'd probably, well...' He carries out a diminutive version of his mouth exercise.

'A tract to be avoided by tennis umpires, I should imagine,' says Mary, brushing her forehead in response to an increase in heart-rate.

'Suppose you're right. I didn't go a bundle on it anyway. The only problem with philosophy is that none of it ever works.' He reaches into his pocket for a handkerchief and blows his nose then, leaning back slightly, examines what's been expelled. Satisfied, he screws the handkerchief back into his jeans. 'By the way,' he says, 'when you've had enough of me just say the word and I'll leave. Not that I want to but ... well, I know I ought to give you some breathing space. Anyway, just say the word.'

She sits down, her toes pressing against the insides of her shoes, a tiredness more profound than it has been all day, yet a dream of thighs wide for youngsters to take mouthfuls like squires in old days with plump game breakfasts, tongues against wishbones and those, Oh, forgive me's, as Martin rears against the window, digs his hands into the arms of her chair and kisses her cheek.

'Sorry,' he mumbles, sitting down again. 'It came over me out of the blue. A voice said, "Kiss her, Martin." So I did. The point's this I suppose. And I have to say it. I love you irrevocably.'

His breath smelt of Toblerone; hers of mushrooms and medication. It hadn't been a kiss in the *Last Tango in Paris* sense of the word. No Marlon, butter or bums. Just dry lips against her skin. She remembers Paul and his inebriated attempts at emulating Marlon – though, searching the fridge, he'd found only Flora margarine.

Martin is jumping up. 'Hey! I've had an idea. How about if we go to the pictures later? Two-and-sixpennies. Kia-Ora. Pearl and Dean. The whole thing. Would you like that? I could buy a paper on the way home, see what's on and give you a ring. What do you think?'

He throws one leg over the other, his jeans lifting slightly to show dark yellow socks. It is apparent that he'll grow into a withered version of what he is now rather than transmogrifying into one of those ageless, indiscriminately plump men panting behind a stout wife.

'And there's something I have to tell you. I've been searching for the words all day. You see, well, if I could – if it was possible – then I'd like to take everything away from you. Yes, that's it. Take everything away. Make you feel sort of nicer than you do. Then I wouldn't mind so much if I didn't see you again, as long as I knew I'd taken everything away.'

China girl as ballerina on varnished boards in an unfurnished room, a pirouette from one wall to the next, her hair drifting outwards in carousel to music and perfumes, the far wall a single mirror of movement, beauty.

'By the same token I'm not expecting you to reciprocate these feelings. How could you? It's just that I have such certainty about you, right here, inside. And I feel good about it. For as long as I can remember I've been a bit like a book no one wants to read, but now...'

He's turning down a corner of himself to mark the place where he's stopped. Mary is creating the romance of China girl against these honeysuckle curtains, an activity to put an end to, Matthew would say, but what does he know? When there are scores of famished senses to explore?

Having considered the matter, Martin unfolds his corner and carries on, 'Now I have purpose, a sense of, well, connection you might say. It's something I haven't experienced before. I remember the afternoon we went to the bread shop. I was waiting, you know, to be disconnected by something you might have said or done, but I wasn't and I haven't been. It's here as much as ever and I'm on the right track. I know I might have mentioned loving you once or twice, but that's just the simplest way of putting the complex parts of this. The only thing I'm worried about is that I can't seem to come across as another man might. I've lain awake thinking it through. It's as if they're all consonants and I'm a vowel.'

She's hungry for peace. Hungry for it. Remembering dawns as rose-coloured apertures to the day; the tang of walking and the tang of expectation. *(The runaway train came over the hill and she blew.)* Her thigh muscles tighten, untighten.

'Oh come on then. I don't suppose it'll do any harm.'

'What do you mean?'

'We'll go to bed.'

He slams his covers shut. 'No, no. I don't think so. Not out of the blue anyway. Sorry, I don't mean I wouldn't want to but I'd rather it came about by itself. I just can't leap into that kind of thing. And anyway you might end up thinking that's been my motive all along. And it hasn't been.'

She's yawning. 'Fine. It was just an idea.'

'Besides, I want you to like me first. You know, me, this.'

'But I don't know you.'

He stands up, thumps to the window. 'That's it. That's it exactly. Don't know me but you'd go to bed with me.'

'Keep your shirt on. Thought you might want to. That's all.'

His hand presses against the window-sill as he shakes his head. 'It's not a case of not wanting to.'

Clouds gathered by wind are cast into the room. China girl, arms polished silver in the light of the moon. She would take Mary's hand, shuffle close and say quiet things. Lie back and peace will come in this blending of darkness, daylight. And then a second dream of an old Chinaman on an emerald hill holding out a crippled hand as Mary settles at his feet and, while looking at a crimson sky, he's whispering monumental stories through the length of a warm day; yet she grows neither weary nor uncomfortable and each of the stories illustrates some simplicity of life. On the bed, the band of China girl's dressing-gown is entirely undone, the whiteness of her abdomen wider now, the edges of her gown caught against her breasts. These are the songs of the universe everyone tries to compose. Mary, China girl, talking with each other, touch as punctuation to difficult sentences, the gown thrown back to unshadow waist and hips, the rise, fall, arcs and hollows, skin beneath fingertips and that old song, 'Everyone's Gone to the Moon'.

'Besides – and I'll be frank,' says Martin, his back to her, 'it's irritating me to realise that everything I've said so far should lead you to think I want to take you to bed. It's not that at all and I'd go round the bend if it was. Can't you see? *It's not that at all.* I've been trying to explain something quite different. Obviously I haven't managed it very well.'

'Just thought it might be easier if we got it out of the way.'

He's thrashing the window-sill with his fingers, a muscular twitch visible at the hinge of his jaw. 'Believe me, it takes every ounce of courage I have to say this, but I hate it. I hate this idea that we should "get it out of the way". Don't ... well, don't ruin this because you can't or don't want to understand. What have I done? There's nothing I want out of you. Nothing. This isn't ... Well, this isn't a ploy for a fuck. Sorry. But I'm sick of ploys for fucks and I'm sick of the idea of fucking for nothing and I want ... a meaning. I really do want a meaning.'

He turns to face her. Behind him, in the far window, the elderly figure rolls its arms in aimless cartwheels.

'Go on. Smile. But you see I want my senses to ... to sense things and then I want something meaningful to develop out of them. A pattern. Something to finally convince me living's not just a whirlpool of chance.' He's lighting a cigarette. 'Sorry to throw all this at you, but I'm not going to give up and I'm not going to fall into... Sorry, but I'm not going to fall into stray bedsheets and make do with what follows. Everywhere you go people are making do with things, getting into the same predicaments, living the same mistakes, and almost all of them end up shopping for the family on Saturday afternoons. Do you know, I was in the hypermarket the other week looking for shoe-polish and there was this chap pushing a trolley through Chilled Meats while his wife ploughed along in front of him tapping at a calculator and he *winked* at me! And that wink was some kind of warning; a warning not to make do with things, a warning not to fall into those stray bedsheets. So I'm not going to do it. Not. Fucking not. Sorry.'

His match has set fire to other matches in the ashtray. Struggling from her chair she crosses the room to tap out the flames with her fingers.

They were milk-white mornings at the hospital, nothing to do but slip out of bed to the crackles of other women's nylon night-gowns and wander downstairs to the dining room, its rectangu-lar space heavy with the sound of 'Red Sails in the Sunset' which David the seadog played first thing to evoke tidal melancholy. As each patient drifted to his or her place in the sea of rexine chairs, he'd slap his hands, welcome them. 'Oh, here she is then. Morning, Mary. How are you coming along? Tell your Uncle David all you know.' In him was the roar of waves in gulleys, noggins of interminable rum and an unspoken yo-ho-ho. Some endured him. Others muttered retaliation. For breakfast, corn-flakes followed by scrambled egg resting in its own grey juice, a slice of bacon, two Italian plum tomatoes. Then tea from two chrome pots, one with sugar but both with the milk already mixed in to save effort and mess. Then chair-time again, each

with his or her favourite for reasons of security and a sense of
changelessness; David swaying from one patient to the next,
drumming up mutinies that never came but he didn't mind,
swinging back to the gramophone to listen and hum, picking
away dead skin from his hands. Only one leg and the joke was
that it had been snapped off by Son of Moby Dick, and then one
morning there was commotion when a Mrs Someone (in for grief
over balding husband fleeing with next-door neighbour) drank a
solution of Vim from a teacup and had to be rinsed at the
General. Otherwise, beautiful mornings, beams of sunlight
weakening the room, picking out individual threads on Thomas's habit as he shuffled through the door, his face in his hands.

'And lo! The fucking monk,' David was apt to cry.

Later she was sitting with Thomas at the back of the laundry as a
late sunshine came limping through the stingers, the air pale
blue and saturated with the scents of mown grass, disinfectant
and something more subtle, yes, a feminine perfume from the
depths of Thomas's godsuit, the bottle gripped firmly between
his concealed legs as he toyed with its neck. She looked between
the laundry roof and the high wall to the smudged green beech-
rise with its dust of undergrowth; she remembers watching the
rise for some minutes, trying to fathom the extent of its colours
and to understand the nature of its serenity, Thomas's voice
woven among her considerations as he related some of his history:
how, just before admission, he'd had a fight with one of the
brethren and now couldn't help laughing over what an incon-
gruous monk he was. 'Being here's probably the Old Fellow's
way of teaching me a lesson,' he was saying, his fingers brushing
the whiteness of the bottle neck. Then he lost patience, snapping
the seal, pouring what he called a 'smidgin' into plastic cups he'd
stolen from the kitchen. Out of habit, but with a smile on his
face, he was raising his cup in both hands to an imaginary altar

before drinking. Mary smiled with him. There was only that moment, grass tickly beneath her thighs which she'd exposed to the warm sun by lifting the hem of her skirt; and they were quaint, well-proportioned but girlish thighs yet she was enjoying them all the same, together with Thomas's good-humoured misery, the call of wood-pigeons and that luminous sky at the undoing of another day. Together they were toasting the last visitor slipping untroubled through the wrought-iron gates in a silver Sierra. Thomas threw back the contents of his cup, tossed it into the grass, lay back and raised his fists to the sky. 'Oh, fuck everything,' he said. The sleeves of his habit were buckling to show a pair of tapioca arms.

Martin is recovering his composure. With a second sniff he returns to the sofa but not to his regal posture; now he's leaning forward but glancing aside as Mary crosses and uncrosses her legs, pulling the denim tighter still. Hmmm, well, perhaps a belly-button filled with cream. Scoop it out. But then he's determined to maintain his spiritual approach, keep these puerile temptations under strict control, beat down a myriad of dangerous instinct which screams needlessly for the ripped-off underwear and raging penetrations. To infatuate his indecision, Mary widens the gap between her knees, the fabric, feel it, skin-tight over damp flesh and the mushrooms reaching him must create the heartburns of a spring pig which comes a-nuzzling through the swill. Forgetting herself, she draws fingers through the moisture as she would do alone. *You'll never put a better bit of butter on your knife.* She wouldn't mind sleeping with everyone on earth just to make sure it's all as pointless as Matthew has said. Then maybe she would settle down to getting better. But in these recesses of reason, and in opposition to what she envisages as a Mother Teresa lifestyle, there's China girl. (At the sign of the Black Horse.) Always one you want but can't have. Always one you daren't have, afraid of the prospect of no longer wanting whatever it is about them. For what would you do with the space previously filled by imagination? Windsurf? Knit? Pearl one, tog two, each pretty jumper a suppressed act of you-know-what? Yes, China girl, the whispers of a green-white sea, a twinkling of pinks high on a rock and she's following the path just ahead of you, her pretty legs against a brilliant blue and for one minute, just one, you might think to yourself: *Jesus, this is splendid.* And Jesus, examining his fingernails with an aplomb associated with saviours, would reply: *Glad you're enjoying it. I was beginning to think people preferred being miserable. Take those Swedish film-makers for example.* And Mary would whisper while gazing first at China girl's soft movements, then the glitter of the sea: *Oh gosh, thanks.* Of course, now and then, it would be nice if China girl turned towards Mary and smiled, otherwise she'd be crazy with anticipation of someone coming along to do a runner with the dream. Snatch! That's the inherent problem with dreams. Banish the anxiety of wanting by *having*, then develop the anxiety of possible loss. Let's think of it: China girl at home sipping camomile tea, reading the paper or running a bath, her toes poking from the bottom of a white woollen dressing-gown. Pretty toes. Toes you'd spend your whole day remembering and there aren't too many you can say *that* about. Next day, waking in blossom sheets, your senses are gentle because China girl hasn't hopped it in the night. She's bringing your tea. Or you're bringing her tea. And for a while you're a fusion of pink-white skins curled on the covers talking nonsenses, China girl nibbling triangles of toast with such beautiful buttery teeth you realise all at once she'll never let you down in restaurants, no matter how much tuna soup she spills down her chin. Then she'll be stroking your hair goodbye as she leaves for work and you'll be contented with that because you're looking forward to the thrill of her homecoming. For the rest of the day you'll serenade the city with your footsteps, floating over shop-windows, stopping by for coffee or sitting on a roundabout at the edge of the park while seagulls seagull above you and you thumb through your *Wednesday Carousel*.

And so the story goes, imagination is a place where only the lonely roam. Martin, wanting another cigarette, strikes a match but jumps as a piece of sulphur lands on his palm. For a few seconds he sucks through his teeth and shakes his hand but otherwise makes no reference to the pain.

She'd been humming Herb Alpert tunes. A humid day, flame-blue cloud gathering in an ominous sky and prickles of calamity among vegetation, crushed farmhouses, solitary oaks. The ditch between road and meadow was clothed in grass and shadows thrown by flowered hawthorn. In the distance was a faint sound as of bowls being rolled along a wooden alley. Thick heat was weighing her down just as the bottle in her right-hand pocket weighted her down. She'd left Peter looking inexplicable on his doorstep and now resented his decision not to go wandering in weather like this when myths of warmth and sunshine take on melodrama, and wakefulness is smothered by thrusts of slumber. Now she hummed Herb Alpert as she turned off the road into a track of deepening shadow and requiems of birdsong; here was the gate where she... And there a crossing of paths remembered not from this lifetime but another, and cathedrals of beech scattering sunlight along moist banks as sweat clung to her temples and forehead. Though she knew it well, the walk was always different from how she remembered it. This particular day she abandoned the familiar route to follow a new path which led, without the ceremony of twists and turns, to a meadowed valley where there was little but irregularly shaped fields and an old stone barn against which she stood, looking out to find that, other than herself and the faint possibility of spies, the earth was deserted, an approaching storm completing her isolation. In the distance a cuckoo sounded as if its monotonous song was made only of sky and fragrance. Pulling open the wooden door she entered the barn and rested on a bed of hay, a single window-shaped snap of sunlight picking out an area of her coat and jeans. Having undressed, she toyed with her bottle for a while till imagination got the better of her and she was unwinding its top, marking a level on the label she wasn't allowed to exceed and following her body with a free hand since it had become indefinite and beautiful in the pale light. Hand across shoulder, down to her elbow, over the flat abdomen, along the top of her thigh to the knee, a sickening in the pit of her stomach calmed by intermittent mouthfuls; her own shape, texture, fragrance, those expected responses, as unexpected as an unfamiliar body would have been, especially when she closed her eyes and conjured up a separate identity for her hand. After a while she put the bottle in a safe place and rolled lengthwise along the bed of hay, its individual stems tickling and scratching her; intimacies of skin stiffening or becoming moist, yet all of it famished in some way.

The barn door opened. There were shadows crossing the hay, the shuffle of tentative steps and then the impatience of one soul gaining entry to another. Afterwards the stranger walked away, taking with him the smell of unpasteurised milk, and she remembers it in bits and pieces, the rattle of his buckle for example as he crept back to the door. She was wiping her thighs dry with handfuls of hay but in so doing created music and the temptation to race after him. Instead, she sprawled on the bales, legs thrown wide, praying to the gentleman with hoofs, the day as a whole butter-yellow, unreasonable, and with her capacity for making things up she was filling in details. He wore wellingtons, she was convinced of that. Removed none of his clothing though he'd pulled a pair of wet jeans to his knees, his tongue filling her mouth, surely. Her abdomen in pain with his fingers, then he was gone. She probably fell asleep for a time. Would have woken up with broken skin, but hunger wouldn't die. She was exploring the barn, slipping repeatedly through that splash of sun or crawling spider-like to the uppermost bale then throwing herself down roly-poly like a child in summer. And though she was more or less obliged to exceed the limit she'd previously marked on the bottle, she supposed this was caused by an underestimation in the first instance, and since the surface of the bottle was cool she rolled it over herself or tucked it in the cleft of her thighs, squeezing all she could. Before long, with thunder overhead, the first full-bodied raindrops were smacking the barn roof and she was wandering as far as she dared through wet fields.

Martin is coughing. 'Ahem. Look, I'm sorry if I lost my temper just now. Bit overheated. Tension and everything. People get tense, don't they, when they're first together, not that I'm assuming you're together with me or anything. Besides, I couldn't bear you to think that I think that, well, you think I just want to take you to bed because not only do I not want to do that (at least not on an impromptu basis) but I've a feeling you don't *really* want to do it either, even though you may have thought you wanted to before, I mean it's natural, isn't it, when you've been ill and you're getting better and your body wants to, well, celebrate and here am I loving you like crazy – so much in fact it's as if I'm going to burst.'

'Mind you clear up after if you do.'

'And if we think of going to bed as the last port-of-call on an ocean voyage, then I want us to arrive there in our good time rather than hopping on a plane to bypass earlier ports, thinking they won't be of any interest. That's what a lot of other people do, isn't it, and they always end up psychically disturbed. I think there must be a mechanism in the human being which prevents him or her enjoying sex for its own sake for very long. I know it's often portrayed in films and stuff as a very desirable thing to do, at least physically, but desire always, well, fades and it's a good idea to have something else up your sleeve just as − if the last port-of-call was Naples − spending your whole holiday there would make you sick of the place. And you know what it's like − right now I'm thinking, "Oh I'd love to hold her hand," but once I've held your hand for a bit I'll be wanting to hold something else and so it goes till you're holding everything and you run out of desire. So I think I'd rather linger in this wanting-your-hand mode for as long as possible, eh? Where's your bathroom by the way?'

That's right. She thumped her fist against the table. Matthew stood calmly by the window saying, 'Of course it's your choice. Do what you like. But you rang me, remember? You wanted it this way. And it's simple. The alternative to recovery is that you go mad or die.'

She was rubbing her hand. *Go mad or die.*

'And to be honest with you, I'm not going to keep pissing about if you change your mind from one minute to the next.'

Nevertheless he touched her shoulder and kissed the top of her head.

'And what was that for?'

'Oh, nothing,' he said.

Martin splashing, coughing, flushing in the bathroom then unbolting the door and wandering to the kitchen.

'A few things need doing in here if you don't mind me saying so,' he calls.

'Yes,' she says, barely loud enough, 'domestically speaking I've been somewhat remiss.'

The kitchen door opens. Mary pushes herself out of the chair and follows Martin outside.

'Ah, there you are,' he says. 'Sorry, but I was just having a nose round. Do you like having noses round? You get a more complete sense of the person, I think. And I see you haven't been one for gardening. This soil needs a good turning over. Have you got a fork? I could come round one afternoon and have a go if you like.'

'We did have one but Paul sold it.'

'Dear me. What sort of chap sells a fork?' He's testing tuffets with the tip of his shoe. 'Once it's been broken up, the frosts will be able to get at it and finish off the job. Important time of year, this.'

Mary has been distracted by the windows up there. The woman, her hair a mess, is pulling aside the bedroom curtains and there's the briefest glimpse of breast as she turns back into the gloom, hauls on her dressing-gown then comes into the kitchen window where she waits by the table, combing her hair. Reaching down, she lifts a sheet of paper and reads it as she combs. 'Hmm, yes, look. The soil under here's plenty good enough.' Perhaps the sheet of paper is something to do with the absent man's work. The woman is throwing her head back in amusement. Turns round and seems to call towards the bed-room. Eventually she's joined by the interloper, maybe naked but at least with nothing on his top. He's reading the piece of paper over the woman's shoulder, laughing with her. It could be that what's written on the paper is intended to make people laugh, or it could be they're laughing not so much at the words as at the person who's written them. Mary's darkened by it all. The man in the window has an olive-coloured chest thick at the breast with black hair. In the midst of reading he kisses the woman's shoulder then, leaning to one side, wets her ear with the tip of his tongue. She shrugs his tickles away till she's finished reading, puts down the paper, twists round and talks to him, though his nose is almost touching hers.

'Yes, we'll soon get this into shape,' says Martin to himself as he takes a last look round and wanders into the kitchen, Mary trailing behind. 'Mind you – and I'm sure you realise this already – I'm not suggesting it's my place to have a go at the garden or trying to, well, get myself involved in your domestic responsibilities. I just want you to know that I'm here if you need me for anything. You mustn't be afraid to ask. I can't help thinking that chap of yours couldn't have been overly stuck on you, otherwise he would have seen to it.'

'Not stuck on *me*, no.'

Dark yellow windows and the shallow delicacy of a winter's day lilting into the living room. A robin on the railings outside. The elderly figure in the background is patting the window-pane with its fist, the city spinning because it spins, and everyone spinning with it, buying and selling because there are things to be bought or sold, loving or being loved because there are those who wish to love and others hankering to be loved. And she's remembering Matthew's most fervent sermon, not about cause because he didn't believe there was a single thing he could put his finger on, but about an element of what he called his 'predisposition'. It had been when he was younger – not much more than a boy, really – and he was waiting to cross the road to the paper shop on an errand for his mum. As his shoe left the kerb he knew what it was to love, he said. Yet it wasn't the kind of love he'd been brought up to expect. It was a love of *being there*, his shoe just about to touch the road surface. Most of all, he knew that nothing would ever enhance that feeling of love. Nothing.

No one. The moment came and went. He sensed it would be pointless searching for a similar thing through people, money or good health. Thereafter the moment haunted him as if it had been intended to strike only once. He looked for it again but as he searched so it receded, till the search became a preoccupation of its own and gradually he forgot the object. The moral of the sermon was that a mystical experience of this type was often cited by his and her kind as a rationalisation for their condition. And if such an experience couldn't be resolved, he argued, it became a handy excuse to continue, one you could depend on when others faltered. 'I used my inability to re-create the experience as a way of remaining outside the general flow,' he said. 'And I dare say you have similar experiences which you're in danger of using. Anyway, what I really want to say is *let go of them*, as I did. Being ordinary, you'll discover, is the greatest dream of all; we only fear ordinariness at first because in the throes of our condition we were incapable of achieving it. But soon you'll relish it and experience the richness of simply being alive.'

She remembers miming an uncertain gratitude.

Now Martin's examining the slopes of her jumper, her whitish socks, the rough tan shoes unstitched here and there, her nails with lines of dirt beneath them and her fingers a delicate yellow where she holds her cigarette. Round her cheekbones is a slight puffiness; her eyes are crimson in the corners as if sadness has predominated. Or maybe she's just very tired. Her legs are in fine proportion, and this is a body with secrecy inherent in its form, a hint (which love can bring) of hidden extras lingering among those uncomplimentary garments. She's shaking slightly, not just in her hands but all over, the tremors (or so it seems) disturbing everything around her and no, there's nothing about her surface to explain his love; neither can it be something in her soul, of which he has no proof... Yet there's connection.

Him and her. And yes, he'd hold her, spend time with her, but mostly as the embodiment, the proof that connection can take place. It hardly matters what she looks like. Yes, he'd enjoy sharing his life with her, though the notion embarrasses some rugby-playing part of himself – some desire to be less romantically convinced in others' eyes, to show a trace more maturity, though he'd be unable to explain quite what the word means. No. He can find no good reason – other than those offered in biblical, parental or social-service quarters (all outsiders, after all) – why this imperative to be with her shouldn't be trusted. That's it, yes. Stay with her. He'd be content to abandon his room and the opportunity for bumping into more capable members of the gender. That's right, throw the whole lot in for this sense of connection, whether it shows him in a ... in a juvenile light or not; pursue these indistinct trails of meaning and, well, *believe* you can love someone for a lifetime without having cause to speculate. Love her as lover, God, friend, father, brother and, yes, Devil too, ho-ho. Then with a smile he'd take her and show her his world as it has been till now. His without-her world. And what a darkening place it has been, he'll tell her. Oh, he's had plenty to get on with but he hasn't felt, you know, quite right, and so he'd embrace this miracle now with no regret. Probably there will be those who'll find amusement in the situation but the joke, surely, is what he's been till now – all that lonesomeness, unshakable even when he was having a supposedly good time in his room late at night or wassailing with a crowd because, well, he hadn't found her, established connection and, with it, his role, value and position in this hurly-burly. OK, he can see she's at a low point of ... of spiritual strength, but that's no problem because at least she'll be starting out on the basis of wanting to comprehend rather than standing astride the world waiting for it or herself to fall below standard. And if he could sleep with her (in the literal sense) he'd lie snug against her back, his nose in her hair, hands loose round her, well, breast, touching *her* hands and then he'd fall into slumber rather than having to seek out its sirens first. By morning he'd be at peace, saying, 'Why, here's Martin and isn't he, all thing considered, a splendid chap?' And he'd love her as he loves her now, each day wanking – sorry, each day *waking* contented; each night nuzzling with her. And, being in love *(smarter than the average bear)* – having proved to himself he *can* be in it – he'd stop worrying and become involved in all manner of worldly things, safe in the knowledge that she was there, understanding and living for the connection too. Then everyone who ever doubted him could piss off. Sorry, but yes – piss off.

Mary scratches the inside of her thigh. 'You're about to lose your ash,' she says.

He flicks it into the ashtray and jumps up, makes a note of her telephone number then, without looking at her, touches her hair.

'Think it's time I made a move. I still don't want to, but sometimes people have to be apart in order to come together again, if you see what I mean. So I'll buy a paper somewhere and give you a ring. You can make your mind up then if you want to come or not.' He's squeezing the tips of his fingers together. 'Strange, this. I keep thinking you've been in this room all by yourself and I've been in mine by myself. And every time I think that, something in me goes, no, that's stupid. Won't say it.' Now his hands are behind his head. 'So presumably you'll be all right here till I ring? I know it's patronising of me to ask, but then, if I didn't you might think me insensitive and, if there's one thing Martin isn't, its *insensitive*, I'd rather you tittered about me behind my back than that you thought me an unmovable lump. Not that I imagine you would for a moment – titter, that is. You don't strike me as a titterer. Anyway, I'll fly now. Don't get up.'

He presents her with a grin which isn't quite a grin and lets himself out, waving as he passes the window. A biscuit. She'll have a biscuit. There's a single Rich Tea in the tin surrounded by crumbs of absent ones, though like the crispbread its snapping days are over. She's in time to watch the farewells of the interloper in the sky who's acquired a Dr Who scarf and is wrapping his arms round the woman as if dying for her, fingers digging into her back and their tongues twiddling one against the other. If they were less acquainted they probably wouldn't dream of sharing spoons, but suddenly it's reasonable to mingle the juices in their mouths. And similar incongruities exist elsewhere. Following a visit to the toilet the world expects you to wash your hands, but if you were to suggest such an action to a companion after an erotic interlude they'd doubtless be offended. The woman in the window breaks free, pecks the man's nose. He pecks her nose to begin with, then nibbles his way to her ear. Subsequently they peck each other's lips. His hands take hold of hers while she rubs her nose against his and he's rubbing his against hers. He needs to take flight before the woman's real lover, husband or whatever he is comes back from wherever he's been. The stranger is cupping the woman's chin in his palm and waggling it. She scrunches up her nose. They fall together, kissing deeply, heads at an angle. It takes all day, ending with a series of minor kisses. *Bob says Opportunity Knocks.* Holding her hand till the last moment, the man moves towards the edge of the window then disappears. As soon as he's out of the way the woman stiffens somewhat, straightening papers on the table, hurrying into the bedroom, patting her hair, looking at her watch, holding a mirror up to her face and sparring with it. Then she becomes a gloom by the bed, adjusting covers, punching pillows. Mary takes her biscuit to the living room, nibbling one side of it into a rough representation of the west coast of England before letting it fall to the floor.

Thomas had been hoping to bring about a minor rebellion, something out of the ordinary, and he'd been right to assume no one would bother him in his civilian clothes, with the added precaution of a hat. From the hospital they caught a bus into the city, then an express coach to the coast. In theory they were free to come and go as they pleased, yet an essential element of the adventure was this outwitting of authority, the semblance of escape. By mid-morning they were stepping down on to a crowded, sand-strewn promenade. At the far side of the road were tea-and-chips cafés, guesthouses with battlements and interrogative curtains, and further on the sky-blue Tropical Pleasuredome, its entrance creeping on to the pavement like a portico with cut-out palm trees as columns, the pink turnstile manned by a plump guy in Bermuda shorts. Mary was slightly to the rear of Thomas, coming to terms with his tight blue jeans, trainers and white T-shirt and speculating as to the contents of the plastic goody-bag hanging from his fingers. To his right – the sea, a narrow beach, the tide fully in but apathetic, its green waves plashing to the sand, exhausted, barely reaching the toes of burnt someones gathered at the water's edge like so much tomato purée, each with their dog, uncle, windbreak and radio. All were turning a blind eye to the dozen or so environmentalists with placards spelling out in crimson the dangers of enteritis or worse from tidal sewage who were nodding respectfully at – but disregarding with as much conviction – the counter-arguments of a sirloin-faced mayor whose task it was to put people's minds at rest about excrement in much the same way as the fictitious mayor of Amity fought against rumours of shark. Thomas was leading her along the beach, searching for a place to settle in peace, the only prospect being to exceed the distance most were prepared to haul their baggage of self-sufficiency. From the rear it was becoming evident that Thomas was an ordinary-looking man, though she'd half expected him to have a disfigurement or be at least bell-shaped when in voluntary exile from the privacy of habit.

For a mile or so they wandered through the sun-and-chicken-leg worshippers till their numbers lessened and Thomas was able to find a sloping rock against which he and Mary could rest in comfort. By now the promenade had ended and they were just outside the town, a field at the back of the sands rising gradually, exposing a rubbled white cliff which, further along, cut off beach from land. Sitting down, Thomas pulled from his goody-bag a bundle of newspaper containing a bottle, two plastic cups and a slim pack of expensive cigarettes. He lodged the cups in the sand and half filled them. A few drinks later, there came moments of camaraderie, brilliance, perception, Thomas fixing his eyes on Mary's hand as she drank, his feet and legs restless.

'I want to tell you something. You promise not to laugh so help you God?'

She raised her cup. 'By all that's holy,' she said.

'Well...' He drained his drink and poured another. 'Christ, I reckon it's going to be a thirsty conversation.' Following an early sip of this next measure, he held the liquid in his mouth, sucking it through his teeth before swallowing. 'Oh fuck. Wish I hadn't started this.'

'Go on.'

'You see, what it is... What I *want* is to be a woman. I mean *really*.'

Mary was dragging her forearm over the sand to make the shape of a thick rainbow. 'I knew there was something.'

'And that's what I've always wanted. It's the first feeling I can remember. At first I drove my parents round the bend keeping on about it. Can't blame the way they reacted, I suppose. Most kids want to be an aircraft pilot or a fireman, don't they? In the end I was so fed up with them ignoring me I decided to keep quiet about it, pretend the feeling wasn't there. And don't even ask about this crazy monk stuff. If I was under analysis some psychological bastard would conclude I was challenging instinct; or at least hiding myself away in that misery of prayer and tranquillity. In most people's eyes, gender's not of prime importance if you're going to take vows and give yourself to God; in fact it's one of the things they imagine you happily abandon. Anyway, that's what I ended up doing, regardless of the reasons. The crazy thing is, I don't even like God very much; at least not the one who so generously created the tackle monks are not required to fish with. But then the God aspect of all this isn't really important. The fact is, I was there day after day with this woman thing beating in me, cocking everything up... Another drink? And there's worse to come. You'd probably assume that if I was a woman in here' – he tapped his chest – 'I'd get along with men, but it's not quite like that because, save for one or two, I can't stand them. And if I'm honest, I'm led inexorably to the opinion I'm not only a woman inside a man, but a lesbian too.' He was pouring a further measure into Mary's cup, raising his own drink, toasting her. 'Now, tell me how you'd go about explaining all *that* to a mother whose only experience of deviance was the discovery of a copy of *Health and Efficiency* in my father's desk? If you take that old cliché about wearing clean underwear in case you're taken to casualty, then that's how my life's been till now and I'm sick of it, literally sick of it. But I'm reaching the stage where I'm not bothering to change my underwear and don't give a damn whether I'm taken to casualty or not. You can probably guess how much harder this is if you're a monk. Everyone expecting me to be serene and have answers to things generally when in fact I'm screwed up to high heaven.' He sipped and smiled. 'Women, you know – not all of them, but in general

– they're like a prayer, like men put right. With a few exceptions, men are sordid incantations by comparison. If ever I've grown fond of a man it's because he's allowed himself his femininity, for want of a better word. Everything's madness, believe me, but madness has some beautiful patterns. Normally I get away with how I am because I'm attracted to women, but the great joke no one seems to catch on to is that I'm attracted to them as another woman. I've prayed to this God I don't like, asking to be melted down and re-created in some more acceptable mould.'

Several more drinks were called for to celebrate, suppress or put aside for the moment these facts and the complete absence of an easy solution. The wind was stinking of steak *au poivre* as Mary turned to watch a couple strolling at the water's edge, both tanned, beautiful and semi-naked, their hands linked and, now and then, their toes kicking at ripples of sea.

'Yes. So either I'm insane or someone's making a big mistake,' Thomas was saying. 'I suppose it's natural that people should prefer to have their sexuality in a pigeonhole even though deep down – if there is a deep down – they're drawn towards both sexes of whatever age and for whatever reason. And though most seem fond of sexual honesty, they usually rear up when it enters forbidden realms. But your body always tells the truth, doesn't it? I remember a particular day, in early summer it was, I was walking in the country by a narrow bridge crossing a waterfall. There was a young girl, what, probably about thirteen, playing in the deep bit to one side of the bridge. As I crossed she stood up. She was wearing a white T-shirt knotted at her midriff. Being wet, it had become semi-transparent. I was saying "Bet you're cold," like a monk, like a parent, like a slipper-wielding uncle, yet there was another part of me praying for the opportunity to touch her, to get into the water with her as if doing so were something natural I'd been aching for. But of course I carried on into the woods. I don't know what all this means. All I know is I keep remembering it as a symbol of the contest I have inside.' He laughed. 'And there you have it, Mary, a screwed-up monk with wide interests plodding in such a narrow direction and with such punitive aims. So let's get pissed.'

He was wearing trunks under his jeans. Undressing, he jiggled into the sea and swam up and down close to the shore, Mary waiting with drink and cigarette, surveying the beach and empty sky, listening to faint radios and the squeals of children in water, then turning to Thomas as he dipped through the green shallows, his body being rolled upwards by incoming waves. In this symphony of fine inebriation she was wishing he'd drown and so find partial satisfaction in the immorals of the deep, given that he'd come so twisted on to an earth where straightness was the prime objective. At this point between sobriety and ineptitude, the afternoon was becoming a masterpiece by Dali perhaps, the beach, headland, brilliant water spilling one into another. Thomas was standing up, showing his stereotypically perfect physique, the swell slipping round his waist, his thighs tightening as he waded in and padded up the sand to claim his towel. She was telling him that whatever he was or whatever he wanted to be was all right with her. He was rubbing his chest with the towel. Shivering...

They walked further, to a clutter of blue rocks reaching into the bay, Thomas hugging his clothes. His chest, thighs, the shadows on his cheeks and chin were beautiful but out of place and, without end, that look in his eyes reminded Mary, though any significance eluded her, of the sounds her mother made on grey afternoons: a duster pushed into corners, the hum-yums of a vacuum-cleaner moving from carpet to floorboard, the chopping of carrots, thuds of a rolling-pin and, often woven among each of these, the monotony of a single voice on *Woman's Hour*.

Thomas was climbing the clutter of rocks. At the top he found
a large slab on which they could catch the full sun, take their
drinks with impunity and make inebriated judgements from on
high. He was adoring her for the afternoon: this warm altar, her
diminishing stink, two plastic cups and a jewellery sea.

(Don't leave your biscuit on the floor, Mrs Worthington.)

Her low-spot, as Matthew called it, came mid-week (if she
remembers correctly), a while before admission to the hospital
and her much later day out with Thomas. She was at home, in
the midst of what the family doctor had called 'an anxiety state' –
though, as such, it was nothing more that a warm, moist but
comfortable bed of cloud into which her mother's head peered
periodically. A distressed head, yet Mary cared nothing for it,
having become inactive, abandoned. Now and then the thought
came to her to cry for help but she didn't know how to say it or
why she should. This curled foetus, relieved a little by medication but still dark to the core, and the piece of sky visible
through that city window was itself a funeral of cloud. Each time
her mother peered in, fragments of the cloud were disturbed and
a voice would say, 'Come on now. Pull yourself together.' The
voice was coming, surely, from satanic lips, yet Mary was
repeating to herself: *This'll teach the twittering bastards.* And this
period had been instigated not by abuse or a sickening world, but
by flames in the garden a while before – an incinerated but silent
time when sleep and concealment had been the only reasonable
thing – but she hadn't been able to sleep properly, drifting
instead in and out of the same period, its flames orange then
yellow, and the snap-crackle of burning wood. Earlier she'd been
at the window but then she'd heard the lock to her bedroom

being forced and had opened her eyes to see her mother and a doctor picking at those clouds. Then another day, maybe the day after, her sheets soaked, the arm of the record-player up so that Cat Stevens sang and sang again, the sky frantic with clouds and, now and then, a rattle of hailstones against the roof.

She was relating what she could remember of this to Thomas as they drank and sunbathed. The theme of her recollection was 'waking unconsciousness', a term she had invented to explain how it was that one moment she could be in bed pulling up covers to hide away from sounds of burning, the next find herself being ushered into an Observation Room without curiosity as to how she'd come to be in one place rather than another. Of the Observation Room itself, she remembered being very hot and seeing, but having no interest in, three beds in a row with hers. One of them contained a periodically hysterical woman. Her mother's face, she recalled, hung for a moment in the frame of the reinforced window. The room wasn't night or day, kind or malevolent. Much later, she was climbing from cloud to find herself at a breakfast table with a bowl of porridge. She was heaving. Later still, there was a fist on a different coloured table – probably not a table at all, but a desk – and a firm voice saying, 'You've a massive problem, young lady. Massive. And the sooner you accept that...' Another time she was listening to 'Red Sails in the Sunset', sipping therapeutic cocoa and inadvertently counting the pit-pot pit-pots of a table-tennis ball.

Matthew will say it's dangerous to think so deeply and with such conviction since the thoughts themselves take on substance till they threaten to depose *now* in favour of *then*. Climbing out of her chair she goes to the kitchen, waits by the window for several minutes wondering what to do then, still indecisive, peels a yellow cloth from the tea-stained draining board, dampens it under the tap and rubs it hard against a patch of ketchup, blood or something which for a long time has been on the tiled floor. *There once was an ugly duckling, with feathers all stubby and…* So what can a person do when she's fucked up, pissed off, bowed down, Your Honour, going under, having run out of games to play, having reached the end of a particular strategy, when all that's left is a faint dislike of being conscious, of being herself, this thing in rags. And when she's run out of illusions, has no icing on her cake, no perfume insidious enough to conceal the stink of her and she's barely even an organism? This is something else, beyond Prince Edward's experience, the world beneath the dignity of theatrical tea-bags. And perhaps one should thank one's lucky stars Tetley don't make contraceptives, letting a greater populace flood out. And as she rubs she's remembering Matthew, raising his chin as if his neck would snap, pulling off his glasses to wipe tears from his eyes, but she wasn't to worry; he hadn't been laughing at her. It had simply struck him how insane she and he were, reaching this terrible juncture without anyone raising a finger to blame it on. By all means, he said, she could lose her temper when the going was rough. She shouldn't worry. Things were going to be fine and she should trust him.

Those words again. And perhaps he does have general solutions for her day, but it's microseconds she needs assistance with, as the red stain diminishes beneath the vigorous yellow cloth and she's already wondering what she'll do when it has completely vanished. What takes place after a stain? Another one? But then what? It's all this simple stuff, these intermediary pastimes, this metronome of life going on, a twist of nausea in the pit of her stomach, mind like a carousel, teeth continually biting lower lip and an inability to breathe comfortably through her nose. Tightness in her chest, a general weakness in her legs, and as she rubs so the smell of mushrooms swills from her jeans and jumper till the telephone rings and her brain, as it were, contracts in response to the sudden noise. She reaches it after seven or eight

117

rings. It's Martin. He's terribly sorry to intrude but he's been wondering how she was. This isn't the call he's going to make later – the one about the pictures, whether they should go or not and, if so, what film they should choose – no, this is an intermediary call. But, all the same, has she any inklings yet as to what her decision is likely to be, in respect of this evening?

'Not yet,' she says. 'But I'm sure I'll have decided by the time your real call comes through.'

'Great! Right then. And, well, how have you been getting along since....?'

'Fine. I'm just cleaning round.'

'Oh, that's good then. Sorry if me ringing up like this annoys you. It was something I found myself doing on the spur of the moment. Has it?'

'What?'

'Annoyed you?'

'A bit, I suppose.'

'God, I'm sorry. The last thing I wanted was... I always try to be, well... Bet you can't guess where I am. I was on my way home and I sort of stopped by in the shopping centre for a cup of coffee. I'm in that booth by the model of the polar bear. Still, I dare say that's of no interest to you. And I don't know whether it was my imagination or not but I'm sure I saw Arthur Mullard just now. Anyway, I'm probably wrong. Tell you what, you get back to your cleaning and I'll give you a ring later. Is that OK with you?'

'Fine.'

'And one last word. I'd just like to say...'

But she's putting the phone down, easing fingers into the waist of her jeans and, yes, one day she'll try roaming the streets for it, if only to have some guy say, 'And what exactly brought you to this? Did you need to pay for a life-saving grandmother operation or is it simply economic pressure? Or lust?' And, yes, to his surprise, just as he's about to lap at the canal it'll be... There, just there, pricking up for him to condemn initially but perhaps create fantasies about later on when he's back two-point-fouring over wholewheat toast. Or, if she can't summon up the courage to roam, perhaps she could knock on China girl's door and be abysmally tongue-tied, saying, 'Excuse me, I don't want you to think I'm generally like this, but I was wondering if I could... You know... And here's everyone expecting consistency. When the most unchanging thing about them is their ... inconsistency!' China girl concurring, saying absolutely this, absolutely that, illustrating points of view with a glass of iced wine. Now Mary's unbuttoning the top of her jeans till the cushions beneath her become a vessel and she's undulating on an oceanic swell, thighs rolling up, down, waist twisting this way, that. *Oh to be in England, now that...* This England, its country-side, pale meadows, valleys roamed by cattle and, in green folds (slinking through watercress and camomile), a silver rivulet clouded with minnows; and beyond these images, a layer of child-days draped in legend, rumour, wrinkled women in sweet-shops among rows of glamorous jars. She'll lift her hips to meet the weight of an imaginary someone, sense the flesh of their thighs flattening against hers. This sift and plash of time following summer rain, its essence a perfume to haunt less peaceful afternoons in woods of misshapen trees and ridges soaked in bluebells. And yes, there was a butcher standing in a shop doorway, his blue stripes wet with the blood of pigs whose melancholy heads hung from meat hooks as he sharpened blade against steel then went to his block to slice chops. An England she recalls of three fruit shops, an eccentric bank manager found guilty of kissing boys, every moment of the world overseen by octogenarians from crumpled almshouse windows, each with a dream gone by of corn-cutting in daisy-days or baskets of bread and cheese in the shade of an elm. Mary rolling from the sofa to the wall against which she presses the soles of her shoes.

She'd been walking with Matthew late one night to shake off melancholy – though he preferred to call her melancholy 'self-pity' and had already given her the meekest of tickings-off about it, acknowledging at the same time how well she'd done to come this far. At eleven they were by the telephone boxes smoking cigarettes. He'd had enough and thought he should get home, but would take her back to the flat first. They had already seen the railings Paul had fallen on to, though his death was the one thing Matthew didn't talk of much since it wasn't encompassed by the scope of her responsibility. A crowd of young men were leaving the King Charles opposite, one of them vomiting against a drainpipe on the building next door. The stink of it turned Mary's stomach as they were passing a few minutes later, though Matthew was grinning at her. The night was cold and fairly pointless. Matthew took her through the bus station as a short-cut. By the shuttered tea-bar a woman with bandaged ankles was singing, 'What a wonderful world'. A poster on the wall behind her showed a suntanned guy in chinos sitting on a jetty in what looked like the tropics. He was enjoying a glass of Bacardi with a few friends, a kind of shake-of-the-head about him as if he couldn't believe just how regular a guy he'd become since drinking it. *I see frenns shakin hanns saying how doo yoo doo.* The old terrorist has been nagging at her guts all day and her head was untangling too quickly, as if she'd lose herself. And whatever identifications Matthew made, there was no suffering as pro-found as her own.

She's rolling sideways to the floor, laughing, jeans half-way down her behind. Crazy to be indisposed with your shoes against a wall, your fingers restricted by a brass-coloured zip. What would royalty have to say? You begin with the idea of creating a structure for your time till something in your head breaks free and pushes you the other way. And the silly thing is that if there are as many of her kind as Matthew claims, then behind closed doors in a million rooms there must be other unzipped women, rolling away from the wall into the first fringes of consciousness only to jump back with cold now and then into familiar excesses. Hmmm. Women rolling away from walls. She returns to the sofa, drifting a hand against the carpet as if she were being punted. Poor Martin should share a flat with Bungle, Zippy and George; allow someone to have their fist up his backside and be operated properly. She'll tidy round. No she won't. Drifting along this threadbare river, fingers impatient, simulating love for the boatman, his sombrero casting a shadow across his face. *How to explain it.* At times her body is white, magnified and functional so she can see individual pores, the roots of single hairs, the discolouration in the depths of her thighs; next it's a romantic undulation of mystery, promise, exhilaration. Yet with each view comes the reminder of mushrooms. She brushes fingers through the pit of it, puts them to her lips, tentatively licks, tasting them as if this holy temple has been laid waste, become overgrown, is nothing now but an autumn woodland, moist crops of fungi poking through humus. Just count to ten and say to yourself: *I am a child of the universe.* Then, looking on the bright side, she could claim to have had some memorable times, experiences beyond the scope of less incapable mortals. *You can get anything you want at Alice's Restaurant.* ('Cepting Alice.) Thousands of them, tunes. It's a tune world. And with each tune, another memory, or so it seems. For example, as she was sunbathing on the rock with Thomas, a change in wind direction brought a faint rendering of the line *Oh, didn't we have a lovely time, the day we went to Bangor.* Thomas's hand was crawling through the space between them and settling over hers as though it would spin a web to capture it. Instead it was lifted and laid against his leg. Moments later, in a series of wriggles, he was pulling off his wet trunks.

She was thinking *Whoops!* as that most superfluous part of him came out of hibernation and stiffened in the afternoon sun. He wouldn't look, shielding his eyes with his forearm instead. *And all for under a pound, you know.* Just afterwards he turned aside and wept, explaining as he did so how much he disliked the need. A part of him would scream to be relieved, then abandon his conscience to face the consequences. In the monastery it had been left to a companion monk to perform the ritual and perhaps she'd be surprised to learn how necessarily and how frequently that need was met among the brethren. No, she said, she wasn't surprised. She figured God wouldn't take away desire, because God wouldn't be looking upon it as anything distasteful, unlike the people who were supposedly loving him.

'Very wise,' puffed Thomas.

'It's probably the vodka,' laughed Mary.

Turning towards her, his trunks still round his knees and his enemy retracting in harmony with a quietening breath, Thomas fumbled in his goody-bag, took out a wad of tissue and wiped her palms and his own belly. Later they climbed down to the edge of the sea, exploring pools left by the receding tide and finding a starfish, a crab, some cockles, a length of rope (which he coiled up and put into his goody-bag) and occasional evidence of the disputed excrement. Back in the centre of the resort they visited a funfair, riding the dodgems, the ghost train and playing on most of the stalls. Thomas won a pink giraffe which he gave to a young boy. There was a loss of sensation in Mary's feet, yet she hung on through the afternoon till it was time for the coach. At the back of her mind someone or something was persistently tempting her to break down. All sparkle had fled from the promenade. They talked over the possibility of not going back to the hospital but it was always a bit of a joke, and a kind of greyness was falling over Thomas because of it. Each time she looked at him she replayed the gluttony with which he'd pumped against her fingers, as if he'd been waiting all his life. As the coach left the town and moved along the centre lane of the motorway, they were overtaken by steams of hatchbacks packed with offspring, dogs, picnic baskets, husbands in shorts, wives with sunglasses nesting in their hair.

Next day Thomas didn't come down for breakfast. She had been made to stay in her nightdress and dressing-gown and was reading an article called 'Twenty Fun Ideas for Left-over Mash' in some magazine when sailor David swung into the day-room, his red face running with sweat. He was telling Sister something in the office, then leading her out of the day-room and up the stone stairs. After several minutes Sister marched back through. The police were first to arrive, followed a moment later by two ambulancemen. David told her Thomas had been taken away by a back door and that one of the policemen had been carrying a length of rope cut away from a magnolia-painted water-pipe in the bathroom. There was a note, too, which David had hidden in his pocket because he didn't see that that kind of thing was anything to do with the law. He slipped it into Mary's hands then swung back to the gramophone.

Thomas's bed was taken by a strangler of rabbits who each day ate a hearty breakfast, admired the view through the large windows, did his ward chores without complaint, slapped his fat, strangly hands on each member of staff as they came on duty and, in the afternoons, settled down with a thumping good Len Deighton. At visiting time he was surrounded by a plump wife carrying flowers and Robertson's Orange Barley Water. She

THE COTONEASTER FACTOR

always wore a pleasant well-I-didn't-kill-the-fucking-rabbits hat with a purple motif.

As soon as she was trusted again and her clothes had been returned, Mary regularly walked with Paul round the circular corridor and together they'd concoct fabulous solutions to the world's crises. The weather, she remembers, was easy, green, with distant church-bells and the thump of ward doors. He admitted he'd taken quite a fancy to her, though she should keep quiet about it because the fuckers didn't like it. Later he was grappling with her at the hospital dance among a cacophony of bright-blazered improbables, many waltzing alone to the rattles of the longstay band, Les Jenkins and the True Note Two. The same evening he was fucking her on the physio steps. In the shreds of an afterglow they shared cigarettes and a half-bottle Paul had smuggled in in anticipation of the event. And though he now realised he should have told her before, there was this matter of his girlfriend Molly.

This won't do, says Aunty Loo. She'll reorganise herself. Start from scratch. Erase another stain in the kitchen, then rest. It's all part of getting life in order. But she supposes she's allowed to take one small thing at a time towards this magnificence. One stain. One cobweb. One shortcoming of character. A bit of vacuuming. Hand-wash one pair of these and, later, a pair of those. Then maybe put 'rubbish bags' down on her unwritten list.

8

ON BEAUTIFUL days there can be beautiful cities, but whether the city is beautiful as an abstract fact no one knows for sure. Those in love swoon along its avenues warmed by that deceitful climate of the soul, while those in pain or difficulty may resent its grandeur in contrast to themselves. In particular Mary remembers coming to after a spell of waking unconsciousness to find herself in a broad unfamiliar street of cold wind and intermittent flakes of sleet which were gathering in her hair. The absolutes of dark had been washed from the road surface, pavement and irregular buildings by lines of street-lights. A few yards ahead of her, above the pavement, hung a large, slightly rocking sign which read 'Mallaney's Mint Marvels', while more or less opposite rose the purple minarets of an Indian takeaway, an olive man with black moustache peering through its crimson curtains as she passed. In a doorway on this side, an Italian-looking guy in a beige overcoat was flicking his lighter at a thick cigarette, his feet apart; and she could think of nothing to do but carry on walking in the direction she'd woken into, silly thing, without her coat. From the street ran a number of side-roads; in them the screams of a cat, the slam of car doors or the bingo conversations of women in high heels. In one window a large poster of – who was it? Billy Graham? Certainly the grin was right. But those roaring over God are never more godless, or so it seemed to her. (*Just twinkle your cloth at this second stain. Your kitchen tiles will be brighter in a flash.*) If – out of all the people in the world he could have picked – God picked Billy Graham, then she doesn't think much of God, nor He much of her, she expects. Billy grinned in the coloured dark, into that milky environment, its street blowing with litter and scampering with cats, rats, maybe foxes in the chuckles of night, and another sound, perhaps the rattle of loose cable against television aerials. The Italian guy's pasta-coloured eyes were following her unsteady approach. The only thing to do when you come awake in a strange place with no immediate details to give you a context is to flick a smile at Italian men as if you understand exactly what the world's about, but she was freezing and quite ridiculous without her coat, and with no money by the feel of her pockets. Another man was overtaking her: a kind of Mr Swindley in three-quarter trenchcoat on his way to penetrate Miss Nugent, his olive skull damp with melted sleet, his shoe tips clicking against the pavement, and above him, 'Mallaney's Mint Marvels' – an inoffensive sign portraying in silhouette a young woman's head and a set of fingers popping a Marvel into her mouth. Loudly, in her head, Mary was singing: *There's a hole in my bucket dear Liza, dear Liza, there's a hole in my bucket, dear Liza, a hole.* The song was continuing without her endorsement and was soon keeping time with her footsteps. As she passed the Italian he took a mouthful of smoke, drew it into his lungs, then cleared his throat through a tube of fingers. To one side of her now stood a maroon public convenience which hissed with the sound of water in pipes. The idea came to her of locking herself in one of its cubicles and spending a while restoring sanity with the bottle she had found dangling from her left hand. *Then fuck it, dear Henry, dear Henry, dear Henry.* Once inside, settled down and partially refreshed, she read and examined what was written and drawn on the wall. Pictures of cocks and hardly any of them the crowing kind.

Labias too, but disembodied like smiles of Al Jolson in his stage make-up. Above the coat hanger on the blue door, the irrefutable statement 'I'd love a big dick NOW. Janet. July 4th' and a reply beneath from Tracy, July 7th, 'How about Mr Van Dyke?' Mary was thinking, *Who wouldn't?* as she settled more comfortably on to the porcelain rim. Later, in calm melancholia, she was pulling the flush for the benefit of listeners-in, unlocking the cubicle · door and examining her face and neck in the cracked mirror above the washbasins. A love-bite there and an inch-long scratch here. From the third cubicle a loud snore and the fidgeting of a body against newspaper. *Ugh! This blob of something needs scraping with a paint knife.* She could remember leaving the flat after a fight with Paul; a bus ride; the looming face of the conductor; then nothing. She'd been telling Paul to sort himself out because in the night he'd spewed up on the eiderdown. As usual when evidence was piled against him, he'd lost his temper, breaking a picture of his mother and making a hole in the wall by throwing a chair against it. He'd been panting in the doorway, his angry hands dangling like a chimp's, his cheeks caved in, his lips blistered. *With what shall I fuck it, dear Liza, dear Liza?* Now she was wiping her mouth with the back of her hand, leaving the toilet and carrying on in the direction she'd been going, if only to avoid the Italian and Mallaney's Mint Marvels. She'd been hoping to reach the end of the long curve in the street but all it led to was a rough copy of what had gone before, this time with a Chinese takeaway and, where Mallaney's Mint Marvels would have been, a greengrocer's quite dark and destitute but for a pyramid of money-off grapefruit covered in mould. Gradually it came to her she was being tracked by three men and a portable tape-player was broadcasting some repetitive song by that Kylie Whatshername, the men indicating in sporadic shouts the type of sex they'd love to have, though whether their shouts referred to Kylie or to herself she wasn't sure — and anyway, the remainder of the bottle had brought calm despite the cold wind, the glooms of newspaper, broken glass, puddles with oil rainbows. The scene was reminding her of one of Peter's poems, intended to symbolise barrenness of heart: 'Oh, misty-kissed and dog fog...' To her left was another poster, this time of the Prime Minister (across it, in aerosol capitals, *MARGARET OF NAZARETH*.) Above Mary now looped the dark red of a railway bridge which carried a track just above the chimney-pots of a massage parlour and a double-fronted second-hand shop stacked with office desks, filing cabinets and tubular chairs.

'Go on. You ask her.'

'Piss off. You do it.'

'Yeah. Then we'll take it in turns.'

Perhaps it was Friday night, when that sort of thing (being indelicate with young ladies) marked the beginning of a successful weekend for some. She seemed to be heading towards the darkened heart of the city where screams would go unheard, but she didn't mind, the pavements blackening perceptibly and the shops more frequently just derelict spaces, empty but for layers of cardboard and unanswered fans of tan envelopes. Now and then a scrap of light fell through an ill-fitting curtain as one half of a head peered round to watch her pass. As for the love-bite, well, she must have been what some would have called a 'dirty little madam', but the earth was a place of infinite tomorrows available for repairs to the spirit. A hand pressed against Mary's shoulder as she was about to step off the pavement to cross a side-street. She turned to see the pale acne'd faces of those three young men, who were fortunately struck dumb by a calm in her countenance and allowed her to escape to a flight of steps which led to the railway station. From there she was able to follow the silver rails till she reached a part of town she recognised. Then memory drew its curtains. She has whole albums of these time snapshots, but no knowledge of their conclusion. The shortest can begin and end with the look on a stranger's face, the thud of metal against metal or the undulating stink of a body above her own. Then there was that damn hold-all. She'd been climbing the steps of a town hall in the early hours but slipped on the wet stone, dropping the hold-all and smashing everything in it. At the top of the steps she sat down and cried. But which town hall? How she got home? Not a clue. Her head a refuse-tip of disconnections. She'd wept for the great waste and, she supposes, for herself as the town-hall clock struck three. And as she lifted the hold-all, a clear liquid dribbled from one corner.

A flash of gratitude perhaps as she climbs to her feet, throws the stained cloth into the sink and steps into the garden for air. The woman in the sky is waiting at her window, smoking a cigarette, restoring composure for when the man comes back. *Her* man. Mary is feigning interest in the surrounding gardens, the floor of her stomach continually swinging open though she's yet to have a panic attack in her own backyard. At the end of the garden, against the fence, stand a regiment of raspberry canes. There are rules about cutting them, but she doesn't remember what they are. Her heart quickens of its own accord and this quickening is accompanied by nausea which, though it has a predominantly physical presence, seems to invade her memory and any contemplation of the future. She hurries indoors, retreats to the living room and curls up on the sofa, her arms wrapped round a cushion. Breathe deep and count to ten. Or stand up and perform an exercise. Don't let it capture you. Looking carefully, the moisture between her legs is visible as a faint darkening against her jeans. All of this from an excess of aperitifs and an undermining of substance by memories, music, freedoms, uncalculated smiles. Now, suddenly, knuckles against the window-pane and the realisation that Molly is outside, waving to her, miming with her lips what Mary suspects is: 'Can I come in?'

9

'CAUGHT YOU out there, didn't I?' Molly's saying as Mary tugs open the door. 'Looked as though you were just about to nod off. Well, you can't now, can you? Hope you don't mind, only we're on strike from work today. The manager's a right pig and there's a rumour going round he sacked one of the women because she complained about his straying hands. Anyway, I was wondering what to do with myself and I was in the shopping centre, so I thought I'd pop round, see how you're getting on. Course, Leo's at work and probably will be till God knows when and I hate being on my own. Don't you? This weather's mad isn't it? Really warm for January.'

Warm for January. Mary's steadying herself against the wall as Molly passes. 'Can't make you a coffee. I've run out of milk.'

In the living room Molly's taking off her coat, then brushing biscuit crumbs from the seat-cushion before sitting down.

'Oh, don't worry about that. I was thinking we might celebrate.' She's laughing, reaching to tap Mary's knee. 'Not that I've come up with a reason yet, but who needs them? Here we are.'

She's pulling a half-bottle of Bacardi from her bag. (Wink.) 'If you ever see Leo, don't let on to him about my sins. He's slightly intolerant when it comes to tippling in the daytime. But I know you were never one to turn your nose up at the chance, so why don't you get some glasses? God knows, you look as though you could do with something. Are you sure you want this fire on? It's a bit stuffy in here.'

A pretty woman with a soft face, mediumly thin legs, traces of girlhood in her eyes and smile. High black shoes, blue jeans and a jumper with three West Highland White terriers, the upper-most one resting on her breasts. A gust of dark brown hair, probably her finest attribute, and Paul's intoxication invariably led him to mention their first dawn together when an enthusiastic Molly had thrown back the covers, took him firmly in her hand and whispered, 'Oh here's my little Billy-o', after which things were never quite right between them. Mary's in the kitchen now, unearthing a pair of glasses from the back of the cupboard where they've been hiding among empty tins of shoe polish, two or three stiff dusters and the plastic packet containing a set of screwdrivers Paul won with muscular dystrophy tickets. She swills a dead spider from one of the glasses, rinses the other and wipes them both on her jumper. The woman in the sky is now leaning through the open window, the breeze picking at her hair as she surveys the city and waits. Perhaps it's an arrangement carried out in his full knowledge.

In the living room, Molly has the bottle in her lap and is fiddling with its top. 'I half expected you to be at the market, though I'm glad you're not because I always felt you were destined for better things. You should get yourself off to night-school. "That one's got her head screwed on," I've always thought. Damn bottles. It's a plot to stop you getting into them.' *Snap!* 'Ah, there we are. Just put the glasses on the floor.' She unwinds the white cap, places it on the arm of the chair and stoops forward.

There was a period of a week or so when Paul hadn't quite got rid of Molly and, in the flamboyant manner he could have when circumstances were right, he summoned the two of them and detailed his predicament, begging them to understand. Everyone had drinks and laughed about it. Paul kept topping up Molly's glass, took Mary into the kitchen and wondered if she'd mind the prospect of three in a bed just this once because it had been one of his dreams. The idea was good enough. Better than Scrabble anyway. In her cups, Molly agreed but later, when the chips and Paul's jeans were down, she declared she was too shy to undress with another woman present and, besides, she had her dignity to consider if this creep who'd led her such a dance was going to give her the elbow. The scenario fell apart.

Bacardi running through the neck of the bottle, swirling into first one glass then the other, slightly thicker than water – which is to be expected if tropical dreams have been mixed in. The familiar smell decorates the room and quite suddenly it's as if the last one was yesterday or just a moment ago. Sitting on the sofa, Mary's finding it difficult to focus and the floor of her stomach still swings open whenever she *thinks* of anything at all.

'Yes, bit of a waste of time all round, that market. The food stalls are OK and you can get some reasonably cheap records, but anything else... You see traders moving in and out practically every day. Then again you're going to have to do something pretty quick if you want to hold on to this place. Now *he's* not around.' She raises her glass to Paul's photo and takes a sip. Giggles. 'I don't know, somehow this is much more fun knowing Leo would hate it. I love him, but he's not exactly Mr Excitement. He's even taken me to operas, can you imagine it? I'm quite happy with him though. When I think about it, excitement's one thing I've had quite enough of for one lifetime.'

The glass waiting on the carpet for Mary fills one corner of the room and even when she looks across to the elderly person's window she can still sense its sparkle. The elderly person is just a dim shape at the far end of the room, adjusting a painting which hangs from the picture-rail.

'Come on. What's up with you? You can't leave it sitting there on the floor.'

Turning her attention away from the window, Mary picks up the glass and rests it on the arm of the sofa, where it catches an image of the gas fire and traces of weakening sunlight, the liquid within responding with colours of its own.

'It's nice to see you looking better. There was a time when I thought ... oh, never mind. We had a woman at work just the same. Went through a really bad patch, having time off and everything. The manager was about to give her the boot, but do you know what happened? She met this chap from Accounts and now, would you believe, she's right as rain. Married him before you could say Jack Spratt. Mind you, I think something prompted an early wedding. Have you managed to get yourself anther man yet?' Laughter. 'Huh, listen to me! Another man! If Paul's all you've had, then you haven't really started. I mean, a woman might have settled with him if it was a choice between him and Worzle Gummidge, but other than that I reckon he was destined for bachelorhood. Wasn't till I met Leo I realised they weren't all like him.' She swings the glass in Paul's direction. 'Still, he's out of the way now, isn't he. Poor sod, but there you are. Surprised you've still got his picture, to be honest. I mean, who'd want to be reminded? Anyway, speaking for myself, I'm glad it's all over. I feel completely different now I'm with Leo. And guess what? We're thinking of buying a house. Me! A house! He is on a pretty good salary. It's quite a shock to us innocents, isn't it, when we realise there are men who not only get a job when they finish their education but actually stick at it and work their way up? When did Paul ever work his way up to

anything, unless it was your Aunt Fanny? What have you done
with his stuff, by the way?'

'Nothing yet. It's all in tomato crates. Might take it to that
charity shop down the road.'

'Good idea. He bought most of it there anyway.'

'That's what I thought. Ashes to ashes.'

'Remember that canary-yellow shirt? Jesus.'

'And the green bellbottoms.'

Molly's laughing as she pushes a palm along her thigh. 'Ah
yes. The green bellbottoms. With screwdriver pockets.'

A tickle betwen Mary's legs which she daren't scratch. (Keep
them crossed to smother mushrooms.) Yes, a definite tickle.
She's wriggling in her seat to scratch it, her fingers dabbling
with the stem of her glass.

Adjusting her position, Molly takes a large sip and shivers.
'Really though, I know I didn't say anything to you at the time
but I was sorry for what happened. On the other hand it wasn't
him I was feeling sorry for. I mean, he made his choices, didn't
he? Something tragic was bound to come along in the end. Ages
before he met you there were some nice things about him – mind
you, I'd have a job to remember what they were now. But
whatever happened came all of a sudden, you know? Like he'd
been taken over by a bad spirit. It took me some time to realise he
wasn't going to get back to normal. Well, the closest ones are
always the last to see the truth, aren't they. It's sad that you had
the worst of it. I wanted to put you off the idea but I didn't think
it was my place. Must admit I was quite relieved when he told
me we weren't going to be together any more. We should just
remember the good times, I suppose.'

Oh yes. Those.

'Leo hasn't got any sympathy for Paul. Nor you, come to that.
Reckons you both could have done with a good kicking. Still,
going to university and everything, he's from a different world.

He's come into the world not knowing the half of what goes on. Says he doesn't like thinking unpleasant things. He does his best to keep his days peaceful, and he loves routine. Want a Sobranie?'

'No thanks.'

'Leo doesn't mind these because he doesn't look at them as being cigarettes. I mean, how could you get cancer from something as pretty as that?'

She's drawing a cigarette from the elegant box. Rests the coloured filter between her lips, lights the tip and inhales.

'You're not drinking.'

'Bit of a stomach upset. Woke up with it.'

'Then that's just what you need. Come on, knock it back.'

'In a minute.'

Perhaps it's there. She can certainly feel its weight slumbering against the forest floor. And she's trying to recall the exact songs of long-gone birds, many of them, singing in the garden as she waited at her window because she couldn't sleep. It was almost four o'clock. She was there listening as they broke the silence. Death didn't matter at all – that's what she decided. And it made no difference which bird sang as long as it did, generation on generation. There would be a future with everyone gone away, birdsong presiding over deserted streets. Still, who can be bothered over people, when it's all she can do to keep awake and when Molly's talking of house ownership, Laura Ashley wallpaper and the possibility of children? In memory the sun's lightening an arc of the horizon then roaming above it, switching off stars, moon, night dreams altogether. And she's remembering them brilliantly – windows upon windows. Besides, wasn't death one of the few times you came alive? When, for a while, you're the only topic of conversation. Your achievements discussed – from your little bits of landscape gardening to your thank-you carriage clock; from your rapture at the first tree house to the tap-taps of your walnut stick along the verandah of your wooden home? Going mad. People who loved you but didn't say weep; while those who didn't like you a bit pretend they did as your scraps are imprisoned or consumed by fire. You shall go to the ball. Your ashes mingle with cinders of a previous cremation and relatives talk of you (quietly in case your spirit can listen in) over sherry. And she's supposing you only matter when you realise you don't matter. And then maybe you spend a lifetime kicking yourself over all the days you've spent in vain attempts at mattering.

'Well, make sure you do. I didn't come to see an old drudge.' Stooping towards the floor, she pours more Bacardi into her glass. 'Besides, I think a toast is called for. Leo's been offered a junior partnership. If he takes it – and I can't see why he wouldn't – I'm going to pack in work and have that baby. It'll be a relief to get off the pill. I'm sure they do things to your head. Keep forgetting to take them anyway. Haven't you ever thought of settling down? I mean, it's nice being free and easy for a bit, but then, thank God, the nesting instinct comes along and does its best to put you right. I reckon you should try a good relationship. Sure it would do wonders for you.' She's shaking her head. 'Yeah, come on, get a nice man, have a few laughs then get stuck in. Make it a well-off man, mind. No point starving for love, is there? Most couples don't like each other much in the long run, so you might as well end up not liking someone with plenty of money.'

The hair on the back of Mary's neck prickling as a high-pitched whistle rips through one ear and partially muffles hearing in the other. Molly is still speaking, though for a minute or more what she has to say is indistinct. Mary's glass shakes slightly as she tips its base and peers into the liquid. *Such dreams there used to be, down there.*

Molly's laughing. 'Just joking, really. I can't see myself falling out with him for a long time. I don't know what it is about him. In fact he reminds me of one of those absent-minded boffins, always preoccupied with something, but at the same time he's charming, you know? Opens doors for me, sends me flowers, stuff like that. I'm fed up with liberated men who aren't in your bed five minutes before they're discussing your gynaecology. He says women are mysteries and he wants to keep it that way. He's clean, tidy, health-conscious and a good listener when he needs to be. There's only one thing I don't really like, but it's nothing awful. Saturday mornings he has this ritual where he gets up, cooks kidneys – ugh – for breakfast and then goes wandering. That's what he calls it, wandering. And I'm not allowed to go with him. He says wandering puts him in touch with living – weird thing to say, but I know he's telling the truth. He wouldn't have the cunning to be unfaithful and in a strange way, that's what I found irritating at 'first. He went wandering and I thought the worst, but it turned out he was doing exactly what he said he was going to do and that got under my skin, you know? I like there to be a bit of danger. Sometimes having a man love you without question can be quite a bind. Anyway, I shouldn't be sitting here complaining, because it's a relief to know where I stand. Not like Paul. He was a lousy example, let's face it. Paul must have affected me because Leo used to say I always looked as if I was preparing myself for bombshells. Suddenly there weren't any. He's great even when we have a row. I thought it was funny at first. He says things like, 'Now, Molly, let's not bother fighting over who's right or wrong. Let's forget it and carry on.' And the longer I'm with him, the more frightened I get over what could have happened to me with Paul. I mean, his temper! And you never knew where he was from one minute to the next or what mood he was going to be in. And I wouldn't have put it past him to phone up from a brothel to check I was being faithful. Got sick of him promising this and that and not doing any of it. The times he said to me, 'Just forgive me this once and I'll never do it again.' Who was the fool, him or me? You catch their sickness, don't you? End up seeing the world through their eyes. You'll probably find this funny, but the thing I like best about Leo is, he's *normal*. In fact he takes even that too far sometimes. Can't remember him giving another woman the eye because it wouldn't *occur* to him. Looking back I must have been round the twist to be with Paul. Just before things got really bad, wherever we were going he made me carry a half-bottle in my handbag for him in case he had one of his panic attacks, and he could explain it all so well, I didn't doubt his reasons for a minute. And there was always the odd moment when he'd be charm itself, and so even when I had doubts I'd think to myself, 'Don't be daft. He's all right.' If the truth were known, I expect half of what was up with you was *him*. All you need now is a Leo, believe me.' She raises her glass with a smile. 'As long as you don't have mine, eh?'

Mary smiles in return.

Considering Molly naked, Leo returning from his wanderings, hauling aside her dressing-gown like Sutherland and Christie in *Don't Look Now*. Early on, Paul made up his mind he was going to write to Donald asking if he'd really had sex with Julie in the name of art because it certainly looked like it, especially in that tiny flash when Donald's mouth was on Julie's pubic hair, which Paul figured was something you couldn't do without provoking a genuine reaction. And you certainly wouldn't be able to jump up at the word 'Cut!' sit down in your actor's chair and have coffee and sandwiches. He didn't write because he couldn't find out where to send the letter, and doubted whether Donald would have told him anyway. It was to be the only mystery in Paul's life. And Mary has her suspicions that Molly doesn't like Leo at all, and won't in a thousand years of opened doors and gentility. She's simply undergoing a short-term seduction by advertisements of rhapsodies in blue. And everyone might say, 'Mary, you're the sexes in turmoil, that's what.' So perhaps she should have hung round with Thomas and made love on blasphemous afternoons in cellars ruined by pews and crucifixes, worshipping – for isn't that what they would have been doing? Pursuing the instincts they'd been granted rather than demeaning them with mouthfuls of valium or praying for an unnatural freedom from them?

The sun fragmenting waves to rhythms of green and blue as Thomas poured another drink for them both. Draining his cup immediately, he was rolling against the sun, unslipping the belt from her jeans. And as she fell through the rock there were birds on crimson mornings and an immaculate root-a-toot-toot. Then he was rolling back, his mouth shining with her moisture.

Firm Molly thighs for childbirth and heavy breasts perhaps for Leo's fantasy, yet she's only in one ripened state in readiness for another of infant suckling, and beyond this flamboyance of limb there must lie an ache for lullaby, Tiggers on the wallpaper, a clown mobile, sterilising fluid, plastic rattles shaped like kangaroos.

'Is this really you, Mary? Come on, drink it for heaven's sake. Loosen up!'

Molly melts into the chair, knees and thighs reaching out, jumper risen a little to show comfortable waist and a flesh more powerful than she will ever be. Mary's picturing the body beneath Leo on Saturday evenings, Molly with high heels to spice up the regular pastime. And here's her unzipped bag – top of a crimson lipstick tube, black comb, pack of coloured tissues, corner of a tampon box; on the chair arm, her pack of Sobranie and the gold-plated lighter. If inclinations were the only prayer, Mary would yawn and move her hands to that moist patch on her jeans, imagining the sea on another warm day, a first toe into effervescent foam, her costume abandoned on the sand. And there should be someone with her, China girl perhaps, no one else available as she wades further in, takes a deep breath, dives beneath the surface. In response the sofa itself becomes liquid and she's sinking into it as Molly looks down from the water's edge, her lips moving but making no sound. Soon a pair of hands break through the surface, slide under Mary's arms, pull her out of the water and settle her down lengthways, a cushion beneath her head.

'Don't worry,' Molly's saying. 'You're all right. Think you just fainted. It's so stuffy in here.'

She's picking Mary's glass off the floor, dabbing at spilt Bacardi with her tissues, replenishing the glass and standing it within reach of Mary's right hand. Now she's laughing.

'I can't afford to have you spilling any more, not at that price.'

Cold flannel on Mary's forehead. 'Lie there for a minute till you've come round properly.' She's still laughing. 'You're supposed to fall down *after* a drink!'

Remembering. The moon as a thin grey segment in a pitch sky and spring winds creaking branches of the apple-tree as she crossed the garden on her way to the stream, not wanting to go but forcing herself, following an angel road to the fence, climbing it, jumping into a meadow of glistening frost. Where she knew the stream to be there lay a fine mist, tangible with cold the moment she entered it and began to undress. Icicles were hanging from the fence on the far bank. She stepped into the water, the pain of it making her want to jump out till voices persuaded her to conquer it, wade deep, throw herself forward. That particular night of segment moon, pushing against the

willow, stroking the root in her fingers, she was beating and
burning from head to toe, wading back to the bank, gathering a
handful of mud on her way then lying down, the crisp grass
thawing under her as she played with mud again and it was like
pulling the devil home as she reached for her lubricated bottle.
Calling him home so she'd be unable to deny him any more. Mud
and glass along her white legs, over her abdomen and breasts till
it came to her she was beautiful and that, all around, there was an
earth sexuality, undersighing the surface of things, pulling her
downwards. Exhausted, prickled by mist but wide awake, she
washed the mud away and made herself lie down a second time,
one knee raised but hanging sideways, an arm on her forehead
and she was watching the dust of stars, the silver fence-posts,
those rumours of eyes among the willows. Each pose she struck
was timed to perfection, the seconds re-counted under her breath
and breath itself adding to the mist. Her best of all: soles of the
feet together, knees thrown apart, arms back, and a moisture
clinging to the hair in her underarms; it hung and tangled there
and she was loving it in a twosome with the rhythmical meadow,
conjuring the weight of its phantoms against her own; an end to
commandments of any kind and prayers for courage to pursue
these rages of spirit.

It has been a while now. Molly zipping her bag, putting on her
coat, kneeling at Mary's side.

'You might not like this but I'm going to run along. Think I'll
give Leo a ring and see if he can snatch a few hours away from the
office. Sorry, but I have a bit of a phobia over things like this and
anyway, I'm sure you'll be fine now. It was the heat, I expect. If I
were you I'd turn off the fire and open the window. It's been
lovely seeing you and, sorry but I've been like this for a while.
Suppose it was Paul really. It... It frightens me. I hate myself,
believe me, but I have to go. Look. To make up for it I've left the

rest of the Bacardi. If you'd had a drop from the start like I said, this probably wouldn't have happened. Just sit there till you feel better. Perhaps you haven't been eating enough or something like that. God, I've fainted more times than I can remember.' She smiles. 'Might even be PMT. I'll pop in another day, shall I? Are you around much? Oh, don't bother now. I'll give you a ring some time. Just look after yourself.'

Giving Mary one of those kisses which are simply cheek against cheek with a smack of lips. Daft things. Then Molly's standing, adjusting herself, going to the living-room door.

'You really ought to come round and see us one evening. I expect Leo would quite like you if you were less of a rumour. Go on, have a drink. It'll do you the world of good. I'll give you a ring.'

She leaves. And as if prompted by her final remark, the telephone breaks the room's ensuing quietness. Hauling herself up, Mary glances at the full glass on the carpet and picks up the receiver. Among crackles she can hear a number of people chanting. Then a single voice outweighs them.

'Hello there. I'll give you three guesses who this is. Sorry about the racket in the background. I was just wondering if you could manage a Spanish film with subtitles. If you're coming, that is. Only I'll tell you why. You see, basically it's a toss-up betwen *Lady and the Tramp*, which I didn't think was quite, you know, *us*, and this Spanish thing I can't pronounce though I remember seeing a good write-up of it and that's confirmed by the paper I've got in front of me. "A fine allegorical exploration of certain aesthetic principles," it says.'

'I'll look forward to it.'

'Or we could forget films and go to that exhibition of waste-culture sculpture by what's-his-name. Everyone's been going on about it.'

'No. The cinema sounds good enough.'

'Right. That's settled. Easy, wasn't it? I won't keep you talking now. Pick you up at, say, seven?'

'Seven will do.'

'Or a quarter to if we're having coffee first. There's a nice place just opposite the pictures.'

'I'll leave it up to you.'

'Well then, I'll tell you what. Let's keep it simple and decide when I reach your place.'

'Yes. See how we feel.'

'Right. See you then, then. Say about twenty-five to seven to be on the safe side? There might be a queue for the film. Can you hear them now?'

'Who?'

'This crowd in the background. Hang on, I'll point the phone at them.'

A short silence.

'Sorry about that. They've decided to have a break. It's just students protesting over grants. I'm still in the shopping centre, see, by the polar bear. I started to go home but the first bus along was packed so I thought I'd stay here. It's not too bad really. I've been sitting by the fountain watching everyone wandering up and down. And guess what? I saw that chicken again, the one advertising free-range eggs. Suddenly I felt quite happy, you know, and I wasn't looking at everyone as if they were better off than me. It's like that, isn't it, loving everyone because you're a little bit in love yourself and you end up buying a bar of plain chocolate or something because you can't remember having had one for a long time. It's the little things. I even had another front-door key cut, you know, simple things like that. And I've been realising the world isn't such a bad place, and that even when it is and you're down to your last joke, there's always the chance someone will come along and...'

With the receiver resting on the cupboard, she can still hear
Martin as she wanders into the kitchen, picks up the remains of
her west-coast-of-England biscuit, switches on the kettle and
switches it off again. Must get some milk. The dark-haired man
has appeared in the window in the sky and now works at his
table. He's pretty remarkable this afternoon, handsome in the
ugly way French men can be. Mary sits on the step, all around
her music, conversation, birdsong. *In the back seat of your car with
Joseph and Emily...* Yes. She would enjoy a period of time – a
whole Sunday morning, say – with China girl, providing everything was just so, the joy of it a dream unwilling to die before
coming true. She supposes it's something to do with collusion.
Being colluded with entirely. A route, but just a route, to being
easy with herself. The man in the sky seems happy enough in his
ignorance, so maybe ignorance is a good idea, none of this self-
interrogation or analysis of situations. Whose idea was it
anyway, that there are some things you can do and some you
shouldn't? And here comes *his* woman, throwing off a black hat,
shaking out her hair, kissing his cheek. He looks glad of the
distraction, turns around and, as usual, presses his head to her
abdomen as if listening for babies. A lens should now zoom in on
the woman's shame and sadness. *That it should come to this after
such an abundance of punting.* She falls into his lap and wraps her
arms round his neck. Probably he's saying, 'And what have you
been doing?' and she's replying, 'Oh I popped to the shops,' or
something like that. They kiss. It's a brief but seductive
Sutherland and Christie kiss, the kind where a couple tend to
think to themselves, *Well, here we go again.* Standing, the woman
brushes down her dress, takes his hand and leans towards the
door. He resists, pointing to his work. She leans further. Then,
all resignation, he follows and they tumble from one window
into another, he undoing her, pausing to kiss bits as he goes
along; she undoing him, pausing to have bits of herself kissed as

she goes along. He unleashes her bra. She's running out of items
to unleash in advance of him. He kisses her ear. She kisses his,
then, as if she's delivering an underarm ball, her cupped hand
swings out of view and he jumps. In response, he tries to force
her breasts into her chest cavity. She's kneeling. He's gazing a
few degrees above the horizontal as her hair slides back and forth
just above the level of the window-sill. Reaching out, he tugs the
curtain closed, more's the pity. Yawning, Mary steps into the
kitchen and slams the door. This is action. Thunderbirds are go.
She's forgotten to turn off the immersion, so may as well have
another bath. Thank God for them, bathrooms. A balm to the
indecisive. Become at least minimally mushroomed for Martin.
As she fills the bath and takes off her clothes, she's listening to
the radio which she has placed on the toilet lid. There's some
kind of satirist performing what's intended to be a really cool and
humorous soliloquy: '... and you might remember that in the
United States they used to have a President. Reagan his name
was, but as senility doesn't complement international decision,
an election took place and a man called something like Bush took
his place. But what's happened to him since, that's what I'd like
to know. I can't stand the silence. [Laughter from an audience on
tape.] We haven't had anyone quip over war for quite a while. It
unnerves me. And you might remember this Gorbachev fellow
who was recently all over town in his armour-plated Lada. His
wife was with him, you know, the one with the communist
jewellery and ...' Switching off, she slides into the water. Feet
are the worst. To be bothered with them when they are so far
away and perform so few meaningful functions in the lives of the
physically inexperienced. Still, if you can get to grips with them,
on this minimal level at least, then you develop a certain pride.
(Managed my feet today. Really! How splendid!) Lying back,
she's drowning her smell in the water. Slithering up, she soaps
all over to make sure, then dipping again. Shame there are no

clean clothes but she'll sniff out the least offensive of them. Not that Martin will care, his Cotoneaster Factor so firmly rooted. Yes. China girl would stand just there by the washbasin, waiting. And as soon as Mary had finished bathing, China girl would lift her foot over the edge of the bath and climb in, kneeling between these very thighs. Helping with ablutions. Men have been in much the same position, their best companions rearing out of the water, purple, brisk, amusing, and you think 'Good heavens! Is that coming up me soon?' And the universe roars with a resounding 'Probably.' Water milky now, concealing secrets – though the phantom of it rears up in its own insubstantial way, twinkling through the surface. Open your mouth wide, this won't hurt a bit. Have it shoot into the back of your throat. Better than Listerine. Raisa and Mikhail too on those bitter Kremlin nights. China girl will have prepared a shallow tray which she'll have filled with thick soapsuds. *Après le bain*, she'll lead Mary to it, invite her to lie lengthwise and, scooping handfuls, will cover her in suds till she is slippery beyond dreams. Kneeling astride her, China girl will then perform an oriental massage using the weight of buttocks and thighs, slithering almost as far down as the mound of Venus, as far up as the fold of breast, and Mary might suffocate with ecstasy as she watches the spine of China girl move towards her, move away, light fingers as forerunners over hips, down oiled thighs like the rhythms of a piston. As a special delight, China girl may move a little further down till she's nesting over the mound, her thighs tightening as she bears down and revolves her hips to stimulate. Then what? For all dreams reach junctions. Well, perhaps China girl will lie lengthwise over Mary, her hands reaching for Mary's feet to grasp her ankles, pulling her body forwards, backwards, the suds as a lubricant, the folds of this and that coming towards Mary's mouth but not quite, not quite reaching. Forget it. Think rather, as Matthew has suggested, of the prayer of St Francis: *Where there is temptation let there be weakness and the cunning to bring dream to realisation.* No. He drummed it into her (Matthew, that is): *Don't give in for this one day.* Must not daydream over Bacardi in the living room. *Put it off for this moment, then the next, for a whole day, then another.* Or end up like Paul – though don't gruesome deaths invariably happen to someone else? We'll all die, yet none of us will. (That's it. Get to grips with these armpits. Shave them when the opportunity comes. Then sweet as anything with nothing for bacteria to dangle from.) Yes, Paul's mother sent a cheque for two hundred quid after the funeral. To pay off anything he owed. Mary used some of it to buy a few drinks. And hid a huge bottle of something for emergencies, though she can't remember where. Now she's reaching over the edge of the bath for the toilet brush, pouring conditioner on to its handle. Doesn't matter much. We're all inhuman after all. As long as no one sees, no one minds. That's what bathrooms are for. Then, afterwards, she'll catch up on that nap. *For in that sleep of death what dreams may come.* Don't let bristles touch the surface, Mrs Worthington. This handle is the only satisfactorily shaped object to hand – not quite thick enough, but there you are; she doesn't suppose Addis took circumference into consideration; and it's sad indictment of men that they are so adequately replaced by a length of light-blue plastic. (Chewier than a fifteen-storey block of flats.) Then China girl would ... would. The problem of dreams endlessly recycling themselves with no dénouement to satisfy the dreamer.

Mary climbs from the bath, wipes herself dry, having a word or two with herself in the mirror, then washing off the toilet brush and going to bed. With curtains drawn, the room is purple too. She's curling into a ball. *Many dreams have been brought to your doorstep, they just lie there and they die there...* Really she should tip the Bacardi down the sink or put it in the airing cupboard just in case. Think of it later. Her knees drawn up, she's soon rocked by those amniotic dreams, a thumb resting on her cheek for a moment before sliding to her lips and pushing quietly between them.

10

THE EARTH-COVERED street is busy with chuck
wagons, horse-drawn carriages, gangsters on foot, the
shadows of passing balloons and women in theatrical
costumes heaving along on ancient bicycles. But as soon as the
unknown sees a sufficient gap he runs to the other pavement,
checking as he does so for money in his pocket. For half a minute
he waits by Centaur Menswear, glancing up and down the street
to ensure there's no one he recognises in the immediate vicinity;
then, reassured, he slips into the supermarket, wandering along
each aisle in sequence with a mesh basket, biding his time till the
area he wishes to reach is empty of customers, whereupon he
whistles his favourite tune and strolls to the correct shelf.
Choosing swiftly, he lays the item in his basket before plucking
other goods from the shelves, among them Kellogg's Frosties, a
bar of nut and raisin chocolate, a bottle of Dandelion and
Burdock and half a pound of tuppeny rice. *So far so good or so fah la
tee doh.* At the check-out (having unloaded the items in ascending
order of significance) he pays in cash, fills a five-pence plastic
bag, wishes the check-out girl, 'Good afternoon,' swanks towards the double-doors then, reaching the pavement, checks the
bag for a tell-tale bulge where the cherished item lies. It's OK.
Passers-by could identify the Frosties, perhaps, but nothing else.
Meanwhile an explosion a hundred yards further down throws

plate-glass, horses and pedestrians across the street, some unlucky ones striking walls and metallic gateways, and at the same time the blast pops windows above them, showering them in splinters. There are balls of black smoke. Screams. Several fire-alarms. Glad of distraction, he turns towards home. Could have been a gas-main, some idiot's protest over furs, electrode-monkeys, or Northern Ireland. With purchase successfully completed, his mood has risen several degrees. He's warmer inside. Indeed, he's gratified to find how similar simple ownership of a substance is to the eventual partaking of it; better in some ways, since at this stage the outcome can be delayed and he can reassure himself that it hasn't happened yet. He's walking quickly, his confidence mildly disturbed at the prospect of flimsy plastic handles snapping under the weight, ruining the game. He won't open his precious, not immediately. It'll stay on his table till darkness comes. It's the sensible decision. Buying it – sensible too, because there's no point trying so persistently to keep away from it when the neighbourhood, the country's full of smilers concealing daggers under their cloaks ready to stick him. The idea of smilers, he remembers, comes from his brief experience of Jacobean tragedy. And weren't those glum times? Anyway, thinking it through, he will reserve the right to buy what he likes. *What he likes.* It's fundamental to a person's life that he should be without fear and, since that right isn't being regarded by anyone, then, yes, he'll do as he pleases when he pleases.

In his twelve-by-twelve room, he takes out the Frosties, rice, chocolate, etcetera, and stuffs them into a rubbish bag. There. His cherished purchase is carried in both hands and placed centrally on the table where it's easy to see as he falls on to his single divan and gives way to a sudden need to cry. Tears for a longer time and more gluttonously than he's ever shed them. But there's decision in him, too: decision that he will not go to pieces like the last time; and this is backed up by the certainty that he now has facts at his fingertips; understands the process. Crying. Perhaps he's done his best to live well though everything around him degenerates into chaos. Too much fear looking him in the face and not one scrap, not one electron of it his fault. The whole thing began with an image, lately taken root in his imagination, of an old, old woman in an armchair. No one thinks to rescue her because she hasn't been taken into account by the strategists. She'll wait there till she dies of cold or hunger or something, then rot in the ruins of her room among the splinters of a chest-of-drawers her husband gave to her on their wedding day and these scattered photos of black-and-white girlhoods. The day after the first appearance of this image he woke to a room full of curtains and sun and said to himself, 'Why, it's irrefutably ridiculous.' But then found himself contriving to believe that an inherent sense of the unlikelihood of it all had somehow been created as an elaborate but effective joke by those same strategists over trays of *hors d'œuvres* at intercontinental cocktail parties — men in buff uniforms tapping shaded areas on maps on the continents, the focus never small enough to include him or, for that matter, the old woman and her reminiscences.

He's watching his purchase as it shines in the afternoon sun. Lifting his thick spectacles to rub the wet from his eyes, he realises there's really no point in waiting for the dark.

11

WAKING TO the telephone, the thump of music and this same smell, her body faint with adrenalin, a sedative dryness in her throat, the room dark. When the ringing stops, she hears the rattle of water against the floor of China girl's shower and the faint *la-la* of her song. She remembers the end of a dream in which the letter-box flapped repeatedly to the arrival of envelopes sufficient to fill the hall. Climbing out of bed, she turns on the light. Her skin is white and pointless somehow, breasts beautiful in the wardrobe mirror, or could be; then that classicism of bone structure beneath jaundiced cheeks. Slightly ill-coloured toes; traces of hair on her shins; abdomen flat if she breathes in the correct fashion; deep, slightly moist navel. *Pluck dark hairs from your nipples with tweezers.* She's throwing back the curtains to check those windows in the sky, the man and woman in their kitchen fully clothed, soft with themselves, nuzzling each other, and perhaps these snaps of light tempt the man to glance at Mary's window where he'd witness this damp but recovering creature. Perhaps not. Closing the curtains, she sorts through her knicker-bag to find the least inclement pair and lays them on the bed for later, unwilling to end this state of importunity. There's a sense in which she should remain unclothed, adopting costume if and when sobriety widens; choosing with care rather than jumping to

152

the whispers of others who may be distracted by continuous skin. Yawning, she falls to the bed, beginning *Our Father which art*, but she would quite like to trespass and be trespassed against. Maybe one day someone will design knickers with stains incorporated so that continuous wear simply adds to their artistic value. She's remembering swans coming into land, Peter's shorts too wide and how other girls often giggled at them. The immemorial sickness of the village. A distant snap of breeze, blood pulsing in her ears as she plays with the hand-mirror. Yes, perhaps morality is a fine thing. Tedious but fine. Wiggle them down, Matthew, for more livid sobriety. Sermons are best left for afterglows. There are reddened lips in the mirror's surface and one never hears of gorillas undergoing psychotherapy and perhaps the one she's seen at the zoo, if he could talk, would say, 'Mary, *you'd* throw barrels at visitors if you were in a cage with bars in front and plate-glass behind. What are you doing, Saturday?' Thighs clenched to hold the mirror steady, this oval of an alternative world it should be possible to slip through as if it were the surface of a silver lake. And she's able to pretend the reflection isn't hers, this wet mouth, whoops, ready to play with monk, cucumber, leather glove, Black & Decker sanding disc, the tongues of the devil to whose tunes one is urged not to jive on the basis that such exhaustive dancing would do a person no good whatsoever. She'll get up when she's good and ready, not before. Upstairs the rattle of the shower comes to an end, floorboards creak as China girl steps out, dries herself, drifts to where her clothes lie. It could speak volumes of living that one person's floor is another's ceiling. If each were made of glass, China girl would be peering at this recumbent body, at the mirror strategically placed and these hands performing Ravel's *Bolero* with equidistant first fingers on bloated nipples. Mary remembers the sound of rain, the gathering of thunderclouds, shadows the merest darkening of colours they fall upon. Yes, the surface of this mirror could be a cinematic experience, taking millions at the box-office, the heroine this aperture from where each slithers into living and to which many turn their waking attention, either growing crusted in denial of it or kneeling as in prayer to fulfil its heavy requirements. And what is this China girl's singing now? She is the most beautiful sound of all, a voice like silken streamers tied to a sycamore (hide in a wardrobe to witness the comings and goings), beauty perpetuated by a refusal to reside in its bloom. Mary's resting hands on the coolness of hips and everyone's lonely, or so it seems, the loneliest being those who claim not to be, each carrying an invisible husk, remembering too the blue of bells from summer towers, a magnolia in springtime, the plop of frogs, an oriental person delivering soul through manipulation of a violin as if each of us had a theme tune but insufficient skill to render it accurately. She'd look up through the glass ceiling to see the pale soles of China girl's feet. Remembers coming-to one Sunday morning in the half-embrace of a man she didn't recognise, his hairstyle and jaw reminiscent of a ballet dancer, her mouth gummed up in dehydration, stomach tight in fear of rousing him. For half an hour she was listening to the birds and assembling from the gloom the contours of the man's furniture, his roof, his discarded clothing, at the same time moving by degrees to the edge of his bed. Happily the sheets were untucked and she could slide to the floor without too much fuss, although finding her own clothes took longer than she'd imagined it might and she stubbed her toe against a blanket box in the process, her face flushing with pain. It was as if each bird in the city was singing as she finally tiptoed down the stairs (avoiding bicycles), fumbled with various security devices on the heavy front door and gained access to the pavement, giggling because warmth and fluency had lingered from the forgotten night before. As she ran she sang the line *Toss me a cigarette, I think there's one in my raincoat*. Didn't stop till she reached a small park where men and dogs were already plodding for papers and milk, and though she could no longer picture the man's face or remember his name, full kisses and the raptures of his wine were coming back to her; in fact, one of those kisses still irritated her leg just above the knee. Resting briefly in the park, she had a cigarette and was inclined to laugh though she thought it inappropriate. What the truth had been she had no idea, but she dimly recalled a darkened room, a crush of silhouettes dancing and a kind of eye-to-eye with someone who later pulled her against a wall and played in the corners of her lips with his tongue. Church-bells lightened the city as she left the park and came home to find Paul sprawled naked on the bed like this, his hand dangling over the side. It must have been near Christmas because there were stretch-marked yellow balloons hanging in one corner. Taking off her coat, she managed to wriggle on to a diagonal bit of bed but couldn't sleep, being so wicked with subterfuge. A while later, Paul was sitting up complaining of a pain over one eye, his belly bloated and the dark chest above vacuum-formed over his rib-cage. Without another word he was climbing out of his pants, throwing back the bit of sheet covering her and tearing off her party clothes till in temper he spotted the mark above her knee and slapped her mouth in case he hadn't been the man to make it. Afterwards, as he lay beside her getting his breath back and pouring himself a little drink, she heard, from Mrs Charles's house next door, several cries for Sebastian intermingled with the more rural dialogues of *The Archers.*

She's getting dressed in the bathroom, spraying each piece of clothing with deodorant before putting it on, folding back the cuffs of her shirt and trying out the coat with the cigarette burn beneath its breast pocket. In the kitchen, she bites Cornwall from her west-coast-of-England biscuit, chewing carefully to avoid any surprise or difficulty to her stomach, and in the living room sits in partial darkness to watch the silver-haired figure in the brightly lit window who stands as a ghost by its fireplace, smoking a large cigar, waiting perhaps to shift from purgatory to peacefulness. A dull orange from the streetlight has captured the Bacardi. Mary's picking up the glass, examining it, sniffing at it. *Innocent, they say, till the moment a trigger is pulled.* An inch or so between this and her lips. Yes. The tropics, that's the place to be. Perhaps city streets cause this disease. Streets and a lack of 'Good afternoon's. Matthew's warned her about these moments of temptation when she should think things through very carefully, and Matthew is an *honourable* man. The glass here, but quite distant. Twists of anticipation in her tissues, contradictory twistings in her spirit. *Just one Cornetto.* As with all dangerous things, its outward appearance is charm itself. 'Drink me.' it's saying, 'drink me.' Shaking her head, she places it back on the floor next to the bottle and Molly's empty glass; looks up at the ceiling, the window, then through to the opposite window where the elderly figure is now watching her, cigar smoke rising to the chandelier.

At first as a shadow against that brilliant window, China girl comes. Mary hides the bottle and glasses in the airing cupboard. Answers a single knock at the door.

'Hi. Hope you don't mind me popping down only I've got some post here for you. It came a few days ago but I forgot.'

Tucked among her syllables, a trace (is it?) of an East Anglian accent, always a surprise when you hear it. She's fidgeting on the doorstep, her eyes fixed on the burn-marked coat.

Mary hears her own voice. 'Come on in for a minute. I'm not doing anything. Well, nothing that's going to influence the future.'

'Thank you.' China girl steps into the hall as Mary struggles to close the door.

'You look as though you're all ready to go out somewhere.'

Mary glances down at her coat, tells China girl of the imminent film as she leads her into the living room, turns on the light and points to the sofa.

'Oh, *that* film. Sorry to tell you this, but it's the worst I've ever seen. I wanted to walk out but Richard – he's a great fan of nonsense – he was really into it, so I had to stick it out to the bitter end.' She's sitting on the edge of the sofa, legs lolling from her black skirt as if they have no bones. Mary has been standing by the window, looking at her three envelopes. With a sigh she screws them up and places them on the cupboard.

'Having said that, there's a raunchy bit. With tomatoes. But I won't spoil it for you. You'll have to wait and see.'

Mary has her first smile. Her first *genuine* one. 'What? Tinned? Fresh?'

'Wait and see.' China girl shifts further on to the sofa. 'Are you going by yourself?'

'Not quite. An old friend. Bumped into him when I was out for a walk. I wasn't doing anything so I thought...'

'Oh, right. Anyway, another reason I came down was to ask if you'd like to come up for a snack, some time. I was going to suggest tonight, but now you're going out...'

Mary sits down. 'Yes, I'd really... That would be nice. Probably wouldn't be able to eat much, though, the state my stomach's in.'

'Doesn't matter, does it? It would be good if you came, that's all. What about tomorrow night?'

Mary looks at the ceiling. 'Well, I haven't made any plans or anything.'

'Come then.'

'Right. That'll be...'

''Bout seven?'

Mary's laughing. 'Everything happens around seven, doesn't it?'

The figure in the opposite window sits down. At best Mary can see only the crown of its silver head and trails of cigar smoke, dense one moment, diminishing the next. Having reached the upright of the sofa, China girl settles against it.

'I should come down more often, I know,' she's saying. 'I've been thinking about it for ages, but it's finding the time. What with work and Richard I hardly seem to have five minutes to think. And how have you been?'

Moisture's trickling to Mary's waist. 'Oh, quite well, on the whole.'

'You're very pale. Hope you don't mind me saying so, but you are. Maybe you shouldn't be going out.'

'Go mad if I stay in much longer.'

China girl's gaze falls easily upon Mary, yet Mary is unable to reciprocate for more than a few seconds at a time, alternating her attention between the cigar-smoking window and the arm of her chair where a chestnut-coloured thread waits to be played with. Even then, it's as if unsavoury histories have settled on her shoulder for the earth to examine. Raising her arms, China girl interlaces her long fingers and rests them on top of her head. She's smiling. Mary waits for what may follow, breathing deeply as Matthew said she should, catching elements of damp, deodorant, mushrooms, Bacardi; momentarily perplexed by what the day has comprised so far, the room a balloon but brittle, the street-night brittle too. She's shivering, and the more she shifts in her chair to conceal them, the more evident her shivers become.

'You had a market stall, didn't you?'

'Yes. Well, we had one jointly. But it wasn't serious. I've given it up for a while.'

'You're lucky. Wish I could get shot of the bank. I've been there three years now and I'm bored stiff with it.' She brushes hair away from her left eye. 'People coming in all day long. Putting money in. Taking it out. The worst of it is being polite. That's rule number one: *Be polite.* Every now and again I want to spit at them. So does everyone else there. You probably wouldn't believe me if I told you the sort of things we say when the doors are closed. Every regular customer has a nickname. Even the manager joins in. He's a good laugh as long as his wife doesn't ring up. But you always know there's a despot lurking underneath.'

Such a beautiful mouth. Mary spotting cobwebs then surveying the ugly walls, the cracked frame containing Paul. Maybe China girl heard the throwings-up, the shouting; saw Billy the Boot coming and going. Then Martin will arrive to screw everything up. And who's Richard?

Mary succumbs to the long thread, pulling it till it snaps. 'I don't think I'm the sort of customer managers like. About two pounds thirty in the black.'

'Oh yeah.' China girl leans sideways, resting her head against her hand. 'You're the worst sort, absolutely. They'd rather you owed them something.'

Mary's on the rim of glasnost but held back by imagination. *Breaking glass. The police. And she'll have been roused by Paul's retching where others had the privilege of a dawn chorus. Your own mess never such a mess as when you visualise it from another's viewpoint.* China girl's the entirely beautiful, if there has to be a symbol of it, and her beauty can infect you, illuminate your ugliness, the shortfalls of what character you possess. And Mary could almost cry, not over China girl specifically, but some discrepancy she's a reminder of, the whole of it, the whole lot. With a deep breath, Mary runs fingers over a dampening forehead.

For an age, it seems, the earth has been exemplified in microcosm by that sunken roundabout in the centre of town where collections of her peers sing, beg or grouch away the afternoons, passers-by walking briskly to avoid infection. Occasionally Billy the Boot – guitar strung over his shoulder and a bottle in his hand – would attempt to engage one of those innocents in mock debate, flaunting a warped wisdom and temporary confidence, slapping one or two on the shoulders for good measure, jeering at their lack of a decent reaction. And as she was weaving through one day, he called out her name and it was as if the whole roundabout turned to look at her. She pretended not to know him, being on her way urgently to one of the department stores not to buy anything but to look for a toilet. Later she found herself at a funfair in the dark, leaning against one of the coloured uprights on the dodgem rink, watching cars pursue one another round the grey arena and there was one silly – as there always is one silly – a cigarette between his teeth, steering with light fingers to give himself airs, swinging the nose of his car close to the toes of a line of girls catcalling from the side while the thunder of *One for the money, two for the road, three to get ready now go cat go* added to the general dream. Mary was smiling at the silly's performance. He had the whole thing wrong. As usual, oily young men were jumping from the back of one moving car to another helping pretties to steer and Mary was in that handkerchief of darkness, an absence of physical feeling, or is it metaphysical? Wondering not so much how she'd come to be there as how she was going to get home again without disintegrating. Above her, couples were roaring against the sky on a Big Dipper, while over there others were being brought to the brink of nausea by a kaleidoscopic Waltzer. Children pulled at the coats of fathers aiming air-rifles at metal ducks while mothers fumbled with purses at the candyfloss stall. Connecting everything, the sound of generators. One of the men on the backs of the dodgems jumped off as he came by and tried seducing her. She was frozen, indifferent. Only the beam she was leaning against prevented her assuming a horizontal position on the floor of the rink. She could feel money in her pocket but was afraid to examine it. 'Come to my caravan,' the man was saying, 'let's have a few drinks, eh?' Then she found herself, the worse for wear, in this glass-and-chrome emporium on a narrow scarlet bunk, a can of beer in her hand and that oily person looming above her, his jeans unzipped. Soon she was behind the duck-shooting gallery with a fortune-teller, her money gone. The fortune-teller – an old Gypsy – was saying, 'There, that's right, my lovey, you bring it all up,' as Mary stooped towards the worn grass. There was a rope stretching from the back of the duck gallery she later tripped over, opening her eyes to see the Gypsy woman's wrinkled ankles. An off-white day again, children tumbling from a blue-and-yellow helter-skelter on to a muddy coconut mat and the Gypsy was trying to fill her with sweet black coffee in a second caravan while an unforeseen husband fiddled with the circular aerial of a black-and-white television. Then it was darker still, Mary wandering among the stalls, ducking under ropes, looking for ways out, but each stall led to another and behind each row of stalls another row and, surrounding them, the larger entertainments... And among it all, disembodied smiles, steaming hot-dogs, criminal fingers, dim inebriates (herself included) pissing in the dark. Once more – or maybe it was still the first time but now in its rightful sequence – she was in the oily man's caravan, her head against a cushion, jeans round her ankles and the motions of him behind her bringing a shudder to what he was saying, followed or preceded by a fist on her shoulder. Later, there was a fight somewhere on a tree-lined green beyond the fair, this same man smacking the jaw of a second. She was thinking she must go home but the dark was sick with colour and music, tough-looking women waggling sets of lucky hoops, then a juggle of walls and streetlights as she ran through town to the sunken roundabout where Billy the Boot and friends were still in conference on a cold bench beneath the lime tree. 'Hey, look at this,' he shouted as he saw her. 'Had a man after her, bet you anything.' Mary was joining in the general bonhomie but couldn't or wouldn't escape. Billy reached into a plastic bag and drew out two bottles of what he called 'the real thing'. Mary noticed that the zip on her jeans was broken and that scarlet knickers were peeping through, but the bottles were being handed round in syncopated rhythms, tops wiped with sleeves, and Billy with his arm round her was giving the flesh between ribs and pelvic bone a good squeeze. 'Mary here hardly thinks of anything else, do you darlin'? Know for a fact you lead that Paul a merry fucking dance. But we're mates, see, and he don't mind me a bit. Share and share alike, that's what he told me.' Someone on the raised shrub-bed was making a fire out of old tomato crates pinched from the back of the supermarket and she remembers newborn flames licking Juanita's feet as Billy pissed high against an evergreen singing 'Yesterday,' the beds round him filled with miniature firs, sprawls of variegated ivy and a large cotoneaster, out of control, its shadows from streetlight providing a scented place for one old woman to sleep, her head resting on a purple handbag. There were darknesses and the crackles of burning wood, Billy giving a lecture to his colleagues on pigs and pigs' ways, panda cars, knees in the groin, crowded cells, pig fists. Afterwards, wiping his mouth, he leaned on Mary's shoulder. 'Listen, beautiful, why don't you and me go somewhere quiet like the Royal for a couple? Just us. Think about it.' She was shaking her head. 'Too many tramps,' she said, rearing up. 'Jesus!' said Billy the Boot. 'Look at this. A pisser with principles.' One or two of the others clapped.

Later still, Mary was at the side of the main carriageway beneath tall buildings with tinted windows and recently cleaned stonework, wondering if she could swing a free ride with a taxi driver. Billy the Boot and friends were an unstable group moving through the precinct singing Lennon songs. She waited some time; could remember the name of her road, though the number escaped her, each one she conjured up seeming like a rehearsal for the truth. Directly outside the entrance to the building opposite stood a bronze of a seaman peering into the night through a telescope. A taxi pulled up. She had to explain she had no money, but the Rasta driving said, 'Don't you worry 'bout that now, darlin'. Jus' climb aboard. But don't get throwin' up now.' She was saying, 'Oh surely not, in a quiz of misunderstanding in which she struggled for comprehension but always fell short. Glancing at her in the rear-view mirror, the man in the multi-coloured hat was advising her to have a good night's sleep and to ease off things for a while, but by then she was losing the name of her road and laughing to herself about it in the back. Didn't dare say, so she told him to stop by a shop full of purple mannequins. He shouted, 'You take care of yourself now,' as he drove away, Mary following leafier streets, seeing no one, humming 'Rock of Ages' till a strangulation in her bowel forced her to coopy down in a gutter and give way, figuring that if anyone should come along they'd be too red-faced to mention it. Then she was back home dressed only in her jumper and curled up in a chair, the clock marking darkness and a nightcap waiting untouched at her fingertips.

These fingertips, twiddling with a cigarette, China girl watching them as if their actions were informative to the spirit, her lips parted, her shoes tapping the rug.

'I'm sorry about what happened to Paul,' she's saying. 'He didn't speak to me much, but, anyway... if ever you need to talk, just come up.'

Mary says, 'Thanks,' to the arm of her chair.

China girl looks around for something to say. 'Do you know what would be nice? A few plants here and there. Nothing expensive. Just a little bit of greenery.'

Mary glances at her then stares out of the window. 'Let's be honest,' she's saying, 'the place is a mess.'

'Oh, it's not too bad. From what I've seen through the window it was like this well before you came along. Tell you what, we could all have a go at it at the weekend. Richard's coming. He could help.' She laughs. 'Sorry, you'll have to forgive me. That's a bit patronising, isn't it?'

'Don't expect I'll be here much longer, anyway. Can't afford it. This other person I know paid a month's rent to tide me over but after that I don't know what's going to happen.' Mary would like to say she'll be busy at the weekend, but most likely she'll be doing the same as she's done today.

'All the same, it would be nice to get it ship-shape. There's nothing wrong with it, basically, is there? It's all superficial.'

Mary winds the broken thread round her finger. 'Nothing but dirt. It's all right. You don't have to avoid the facts. Plain old dirt.'

The darkest eyes has China girl, barely a distinction between pupil and iris; over her white skin a flush of red from the bulb, orange from the streetlight. A smile to immediately weaken you. Thin magnetic limbs. Hand always ready to push back strands of offending hair.

'OK, I agree. We'll call it dirt.'

To avoid China girl's eyes, Mary stands and takes off her coat, throwing it over the back of her chair before sitting down again, her hands shaking. She crosses her legs, puts out her cigarette and traps her fingers between her knees as China girl, having paused to stifle a yawn, continues to speculate. 'The garden could be quite nice too, with a few tubs here and there. But, if you're not staying...'

'Yes. Paul was always going to do it, but dying stood in his way.'

China girl waits for Mary to smile before smiling herself.

'We were both a complete shambles, if you must know. Anyway, you'd probably guessed that. Sorry, I didn't want to mention it but there's no point keeping the secret when you had a grandstand view.'

'Well, there *were* clues. Like that night in the garden. Remember? About eleven o'clock it was, and you were out there in your nightie and wellingtons digging a hole by those old raspberry canes. You were burying a big bottle or something.'

'So *that's* where I put it. I was thinking of it earlier.'

China girl leans forward. 'Why were you burying it? What was the point?'

'Oh, I just wanted to keep it a secret, that's all.'

'But you were on your own by then.'

'Yes.'

'So who were you hiding it from?'

'I don't know.'

'That's really weird.'

'It is, isn't it.'

Though Mary tries not to join in for fear of crying, China girl has fallen sideways, laughing, it seems, till she'll die, her legs lifting from the floor, body twisting at the waist, her face showered in black hair; and as she swings upright again the hair swings with her, the colours of her skin having deepened, her movement unearthing traces of a white neck, an ear, the glint of gold. Mary's mouth and throat tighten with an awkwardness verging on hostility as China girl, to rearrange herself, drops her head to her knees and lifts it quickly, the hair fanning out before falling into place. Pulling hands free of her legs, Mary grips the chair as the room swings to the right and back again and her heart plays an unusual rhythm in response.

China girl's apologising, her head tilted inquisitively. 'I shouldn't be laughing. Are you all right?'

To counteract vertigo, Mary unhooks her left hand, squeezes her ear-lobe and for the first time looks at China girl without having to turn away.

'Well, I probably will be, but I don't feel much like a spring lamb at the moment.' There. Put it perfectly. 'The room's gone out of shape or something.'

Swinging to her feet, China girl comes to kneel at the side of Mary's chair. 'Out of shape?'

'I don't know how else to put it.'

'Perhaps it's 'flu. You look a bit damp.'

Any movement of Mary's head prompts movement in the room, while the furniture has become swollen, grotesque. The proximity of China girls weighs heavily against her cheek and she jumps when that soft hand rests against her shoulder.

'Can I get you anything?'

'A draught of hemlock should do it.'

'You look terrified.'

'It might come out like terror, but it's probably the wisdom of centuries.'

China girl shuffles around to face Mary, her hand taking an age to reach and stroke this unkempt hair. Though Mary wouldn't describe herself as grief-stricken, her eyes have begun to water and she's afraid China girl might jump to a false conclusion. A grief-stricken child falling through realms of abject fantasy, Mary's drinking perfumes from China girl and China girl's life.

'Shall I get you an aspirin?'

Mary shakes her head once, the room responding in kind but taking some time to rock itself to a standstill. China girl is reaching forward to rest her head against Mary's shoulder. 'There was I laughing, and now this,' she says.

And now this, China girl's ebony hair brushing Mary's cheek

as the inebriate twists to kiss it and the room sways in return. Kissing hair, as though her mouth had acted of its own volition. It's called letting ecstasies get the better of you in the foothills of recovery. What nonsense. Such neat approximations come to her continually and what blame can be attached when a living perfume kneels before you, light from a red bulb hanging in its hair, its white face shifting back to look into your eyes?

'I could fetch some brandy from upstairs if that would do any good. Richard gave me some for Christmas. I haven't opened it yet.'

'No, don't bother. It'll pass in a minute.'

China girl's palm touches Mary's brow then follows a line from there to her ear.

'You're very warm.'

'Am I?'

'Yes, and you're definitely sweating.'

Definitely sweating. Oh it's not beauty so much as something which perplexes you, an attitude you wish to examine at length in the hope of realising a cause other than this gathering of commonplace features or a certain something in her eyes; the reaching deepnesses of them.

'Yes, I can feel it.'

China girl's mouth is six or seven inches away, something on her breath, toothpaste maybe. Her teeth, regular and clean, her tongue smooth as if it has never experienced excess of any kind.

'You should be in bed.'

'I've been twice already. Anyway, it's nothing like that. Believe me, in some ways it's a marked improvement. I'm fine.'

China girl's hand runs over Mary's shoulder, down her arm to her elbow.

'You know best.'

Her hand has left trails of irritation behind. Mary can smell the warmth of her shower, the soap she used, the sweetnesses of talcum powder, and all the while there's an imagination of her waist, the tucks of skin in her underarms, the shallow recess of her spine ending in a swathe maybe of dark down.

A movement of the room pushes Mary towards China girl's mouth as a street-shadow brushes the wall.

Rat-a-tat-tat. Pause. Tat-tat.

China girl turns away to look at the window. 'Was that the door?' She turns back, brushing Mary's wet cheek with her hand. 'Shall I answer it?'

Mary wipes her mouth and nose with the sleeve of her jumper. 'Suppose you'd better. It'll only be Martin. And he'll have seen us anyway.'

China girl stands, looks at Mary for a moment and then goes into the hall. A few 'Oh hello's, 'Yes's and 'Right then's till Martin slithers into the living room, a bunch of premature daffodils in his arms. China girl follows, but waits by the door.

'Here I am then, dead on time, well, nearly. Didn't realise they locked up the shopping centre at half-past. So I thought you wouldn't mind if I came straight round. Are you all set?' He looks at China girl. 'I hope I'm not levering you out.'

China girl's in the doorway, an expression of *something* in her eyes. 'No, of course not.' She looks over Martin's shoulder. 'Don't forget then,' she's saying. 'Tomorrow night. About seven.' Raising her palm, she leaves. Martin raises his. The front door slams, then her shadow can be seen tapping up the steps.

'Thought a few flowers might cheer up your room.' The daffodils fall into Mary's lap. 'Have you got a vase or something?'

Bowing her head, Mary rubs her temple. 'You'll probably find one under the sink.'

He fetches it. A green, twisted one he's half filled with water. Gingerly lifting the flowers from her lap, he takes off the paper, pushes the stems into the water and minutely arranges them.

It's coming to her now. Once unearthing that same vase for an outrageous whisky-mac.

'Where shall I put them? On the mantel? The window-sill?'

'Mantel.'

On the mantel is an extraordinary place for daffodils. Matthew promised that by the first yellow bloom she'd be as good as new. Almost. And when that time came then everything else would be a bad dream. *The past etcetera.* Yes, that's how he put it. *The past etcetera.* But probably foreign daffodils don't count. Martin places them with great care, as if his future depends on the outcome, standing back to admire them in what he would probably call 'their entire context'. Satisfied, he sits on the sofa in a flurry of hands and knees.

'I have a feeling I arrived at a bad time. Knew it the moment I came through the door. Sorry. Who was the, ah, young person, by the way?'

'China girl. From upstairs.'

Martin laughs. 'Hmmm, I see you've been inspired by David Bowie. You mean Chinese.'

Mary's adamant. 'No. *China.* China girl.'

Martin crosses his legs and waggles his foot. 'Yes, well, she's rather beautiful, isn't she? Though of course, it goes without saying that...'

'Don't then.'

He claps his hands, lifts his knee. 'But from what I've heard – perhaps I shouldn't say it – anyway, from what I've heard, one of the drawbacks of the Oriental woman is her short, well, shelf-life.'

A sprig of laughter falls from his mouth as Mary climbs to her feet, rubs her eyes and gathers her coat.

Martin yawns with what's probably misdirected desire. 'Oh, right. Are we off then? What do you want to do? Stop for coffee on the way?'

'You can decide.'

'Ah,' he says, scratching deliberation into his hair. She spots an onyx of sweat in his armpit. 'Well, like I told you, there's a nice place opposite the pictures. Everyone goes there. I heard someone say Bamber Gascoigne showed up the other night.'

'Bamber Gascoigne!' Her attempts at emphasis have gone awry. She'd meant to say 'Bamber *Gascoigne.*'

Martin attempts to relax his lower jaw and in so doing resembles Neanderthal Man. 'Yeah, I bump into Bamber all over the place. Whether you see him on TV or in real life, he always gives you the impression he's scrubbed his nails that very morning. And I used to love the way he'd tell students on *University Challenge* the right answer as if he'd known it all along. I've often thought that if you were asked to state what he does for a living, you'd probably end up saying, "Well, he's being Bamber Gascoigne." And that can make me me feel queasy about myself because I know I'll only ever get paid for *doing* rather than *being.* Anyway, we could have a coffee there then shoot across. All right?'

She's saying, 'Yes,' though a barrier has fallen between the night outside and this tentative sanctuary, Martin pulling at each of his fingers in turn to crack the joints before adjusting his leather jacket and faking a yawn.

She's in the bathroom, blowing her nose, spraying herself with deodorant a second time, wrapping a tablet in a piece of tissue and tucking it into her coat pocket. She can hear the tap of Martin's shoes against tiles in the hall and the weight of China girl's movements on the floor above.

12

FIGURE IN the window keeping watch as they leave the flat, a knitted skullcap resting on its silver crown, its blemished palm flattened against glass which, being old and under pressure, warps the person's features, bends the streaks of streetlight striking it. He or she is smiling, or is it despair? As they come into the main road, Martin adopts the sword-side of her, his hands itching at the prospect of once more holding hers. Traffic still crawls in both directions, headlamps flirting with the tarmac. In the beginning God created wistfulness, this discrepancy between possibles and the silhouettes of office shoes weaving through traffic from one side of the street to the other. Her vertigo – a name she's adopted through lack of information – has subsided a little and she's figuring she's been an absolute twerp over China girl and won't know quite how to go for the snack tomorrow night without breaking up pink and apologetic. Cold evening, a reasonably heavy population in the street and though each car makes no specific sound there is an overall Stravinsky of them ticking over, accelerating, sounding horns. To her right is the illuminated Danish restaurant, a familiar couple at a table close to the window, their two books – Proust and *Marmosets* – one on top of the other, but by the couple's eyes it would seem rapture has this time captured them over forkfuls of flaked pastry and, whatever irrefutable love may be, he has it and she has it; it's something in the man's faint smile and something in the woman's eyes. Between them are a table-lamp and scarlet serviettes.

Martin laughs to himself. 'No, they haven't quite caught on, have they? Baked potatoes, I mean.'

He's referring to Stuffed Edwards, a takeaway next to the Danish restaurant where a woman in red stands behind the chrome-and-glass counter flicking through a magazine.

'The times I've lain in bed thinking about the poor souls who cook up ideas for places like this. You can picture them, can't you, dressing up to the nines, bouncing into the bank and the manager sitting them down saying, "And what can I do for you?" and whoever-they-are saying, "Well, we've got this really great idea about baked potatoes." '

The woman's wearing a red-and-white cardboard cap with *Stuffed Edwards* printed across the front. On the aluminium base of the counter are a dozen plastic tubs containing the various fillings. Maybe it hasn't worked because of the potato's humble associations, disguised when in chip form but frankly blatant when in unwieldy lumps like that, and anyway you can't really eat them as you're walking along, not as comfortably as chips. Once or twice you might buy one on the way home, out of curiosity, carry it to your place of residence, mindful that tipping it from the horizontal will result in a displacement of filling; but when you open the box and fetch your knife and fork, you can't help knowing it's just a potato whatever's been poked into the top of it, and then perhaps your world diminishes a little. And as eating it holds no real surprise, your mind probably drifts away to someone you loved and lost or to other dangers like Dan Quayle and hepatitis B; and, as if it was inevitable the moment you bought the potato, you become introspective and melancholy. In the morning of course, clearing up your sticky kitchen, you have just a hollowed-out potato-skin and red eyes from bad dreams over Dan.

'Sorry. It's mean of me. I should have asked if you wanted one. They do them with chilli con carne.'

Stomach looping the loop.

'No thank you, Martin. I've eaten anyway. But you go ahead if you want one.'

He's shaking his head. 'Oh no, I don't fancy it at all. Just wondered if you did.'

'I don't like them. They're too...'

'Don't tell me. *Potato-ish*, that's what you were going to say.' He's laughing again. 'Hey! I wonder if they do them with mashed potato fillings? *That's* the kind of thing I think about at night. Like bread sandwiches. I mean, things would reach a kind of crescendo, wouldn't they, if you could have baked potatoes with mashed-potato filling. Cannibalism almost.'

'Almost,' says Mary.

An insubstantial memory of running along here – though in that direction rather than this – a sudden heavy shower throwing up dust from the pavement then – and perhaps it isn't even true – going into the shoe shop over there to ask for a cup of coffee. If it happened then, yes, that's definitely the one: SANDERSONS. In small lettering underneath: *Footwear for the Discriminating*. Selling thousands of pairs to South Africa. She's slipping her arm through Martin's to fight off the pull of agoraphobia. He turns to her and winks; breathes in deeply as if to smell the night. Yes, SANDERSONS.... A breathless Mary pushing open the glass door, interrupting the assistant to beg a cup of coffee, and the assistant's voice saying 'But madam, this is a shoe shop.' Mary saddened by the superfluity of this statement, swinging round and accidentally knocking to the floor a carousel of Countryside Casuals. If it did happen, then it must have been the day she left hospital. Paul had been let out the week before and the idea had been for her to go and stay with him for 'larks'. His conviction had been that most of her troubles were to do with her mother so she wrote to her, listing her reasons for wanting to move in with him, one of them being 'to gain a modicum of independence'. But, having stopped for a drink on the way, form took a turn for the worse and somewhere in the eye of the spiral which followed she must have gone round the twist in SANDERSONS. *But, madam, this is a shoe shop.*

Maybe this is high blood-pressure, stress or a defective heart; some ailment to justify a telescopic street, the grandeur of Martin's shoes and juries of Kafka people laughing as, with right hand tucking over hers, he guides her through the traffic to a small white place she's seen many times called The Coffee Bar, a silhouette of a Beryl Cook backyard painted on the window. Martin opening the door for her, scanning the small round tables for Bamber then leading her to a dark corner where he settles her down on a bentwood chair, his fingers fluttering at a waitress close by. George Melly *rambam-balam-bams* among hums of upwardly mobile conversation. China girl was a few inches away and one screwed it up, didn't one? Who could love a drunk with a warped imagination? Then Martin knocking at the door. Not that she would have done anything because ordinary people haven't read the scripts of her fantasies; fantasies designed, most likely, not to come true or they wouldn't be fantasies any more. And you'd be up a gum tree. *Rambam-balam-bam-choo.* Dreams gone wicked. China girl, her thin eyebrows, and it was most noticeable that her facial expressions could rearrange themselves in an instant and such beauty lay in witnessing the flash of one look to another, like wind against corn. Yes, Martin would like a frothy coffee with sprinkled chocolate and ... what does Mary want?

'Anything.'

'Ah. Well, that's two of those coffees with the...'

She's remembering the blackbird, its fruit-song singular at dawn, and supposes it would be timely if one of Matthew's gods breathed peace into her and ended this unjust sensation. And so confident was Matthew as he sermoned, she hadn't doubted he'd had an awakening of his own, though she didn't like to dream of such a thing for herself since when the beautiful is anticipated it stops being beautiful and you become indifferent to it before you realise you have it, almost. 'You can't anticipate recovery,' he said. All the same it was a comfort listening to a fool speaking colourfully of the world. Not that he was lily-livered, wet or anything, but he'd allowed himself a certain rhapsody over freedom, those un-hungover mornings, the subtleties of form in everyday things. And he'd been quite sure of the very moment his old self had cracked and fallen away. He'd woken one day and had been looking at a bunch of dried flowers on his bedside table – told her he'd suddenly become aware of them, though outside wind was moaning and fat (his word) raindrops were striking his window.

'It came to me everything was simple,' he said.

She was laughing as he pulled himself forward and adjusted his spectacles.

'It's true. Everything *is* simple.'

Then, coming to her chair, he squeezed her till the pen in his top pocket began to dig into her chin. And though it wasn't easy from that predicament, she managed to mumble, 'Let's hope you're right,' in anticipation of his letting go of her, but he squeezed all the more as if his arms were wrapping round her several times, her own arms hanging bloodless at her sides. And she remembers thinking, *He smells of gammon.*

175

'Ah, here we are then. Thank you.' The waitress ignores Martin as she places the coffees on the table. He twists his cup for a few thoughtful seconds before looking up at Mary.

'The more I think about it, the more I find it harder to believe, you know, that you're here with me and that I feel at ease and excited at the same time. It's a pleasant café. I'm taking someone I'm crazy about to the pictures, the East Germans are going democratic, George Melly's singing. It's been a day I'll remember for the rest of my – well, for a long time. I love your perfume, by the way. What's it called?'

'Addiction.'

'Beautiful. You see, I love this café and I love you to smithereens, so there's no point, is there, in my not telling the truth? I mean, wherever you go and whatever you do, you come across people holding back and I don't want to do it. If you hold back you can't really be yourself, can you? It's like being in disguise. When a person – a man, say – has glimpsed some sort of truth, it's an immense relief if he sees it becoming, well, truer and truer. The only problem I have is that whenever I look at you I want to say silly things like "I feel I've known you all my life," but I'm sure if I did I'd start coming across as, well, a bit of a drip.'

Mary sculpting her froth: 'Oh surely not.'

'Like everyone else I want to be regarded as cool and – what's the word? – hip? Yes, I want to be hip, but with you around it's not so easy. I'm so taken with you I'd like to kneel down at your feet and everything.'

'You're not going to, are you?'

He's laughing. 'No, ha, I didn't mean *really*. Spiritually, that's what I meant. It's long been a theory of mine that those tough-looking guys you see in catalogues are tough simply because they haven't come across the right woman. And that when they do they'll be as, well, as helpless as I am. Anyway, I'm sorry for landing all this on you, but I can't remember ever having such a significant day. A bit like Rabbit in *The House at Pooh Corner.*'

'No, that was *busy*. Rabbit's busy day.'

'Fair enough. But you can see the principle. I woke up this morning and did what I always do: had toast, fed the hamster, strolled to the bread shop. And just hours later, here I am, inextricably different.'

Her fingers won't meet through the handle of the cup and the surface of her coffee trembles. Surrounding Martin's voice are the conversations of people at tables, some with hands linked across the pine, others who've grown or been eased out of mystery, tapping spoons to the *rambam-balam-bams* or pushing back on two legs of their chairs. One of them – the bloke with the creased jacket – is doing his damnedest to entertain the woman and ginger-haired boy sitting opposite him. 'Yes,' he's saying, 'and then this voice was coming over the intercom saying, "First-class passengers may like to proceed to the buffet where your steward is now serving our Hawaiian grill." I was in fits. Can you imagine it? Hawaiian grill at a hundred miles an hour through Didcot?' The woman half smiles at the surface of the table as the bored ginger-haired boy flicks the sugar with his spoon, and the woman (somehow from the corner of her mouth and without damaging her smile) whispers,' You're heading for trouble, Benjamin.'

'And I've made a decision, I'm going to be honest with you. It seems to me so many romantic empires reach destruction through the pressures of deceit. (That was good, wasn't it?) For example, I can't pretend I haven't met other, you know, women and that, but it's never been more than walking out really and it wasn't till I saw you I realised what was what, as though I'd been wandering through a gallery of scribbles not knowing there were Constables just round the corner. Besides, any other relationships I've had have been – well in retrospect – superficial, whereas everything about you comes from beneath the surface. Till last year I was friends with a girl called Rebecca, but nothing quite flowered and she was so practical, if you know what I mean. She didn't seem to have a soul. Even her friends called her Pecky Becky.' Leaning forward, he raises his cup an inch or so, then lowers it without drinking. 'Oh, I liked her well enough, but she soon tired of me even though I took her all over, to the zoo and places like that. Ah, sometimes I sit down and I think what a strange world it is. Do you do that? Sit down and think what a strange world it is? Take the other day. I was in the supermarket looking for milk. There was a huge cold-cabinet at the far end with the cartons stacked in it. You'll laugh. There was semi-skimmed, fully skimmed, high-calcium low-fat, something called organic milk in a green plastic bottle, but as it turned out, they'd run out of milk, ordinary milk. Can you see my point?'

'Benjamin! How many times have I got to tell you? You don't flick sugar.'

Yes. Come to think of it, it must have been the same night because she was particularly cold as she tiptoed back up the stairs to the landing, happened to glance to the right through a partially opened bedroom door and saw her father dressed in stockings and white cotton underwear standing like a statuette at the edge of the double bed while her half-naked mother wrestled to pull over her own fat legs a pair of his work-trousers, black with grey stripes. His white backside was blooming through the underwear and the back of his thighs, black hairs and all, were squashed beneath the stockings like bank-robbers' faces. As she moved round, Mary had a side view of the unmuscled scroll of his belly hanging over a black suspender-belt. There was no point, she supposes, pretending or keeping secrets that late in marriage. He was still wearing his favourite slippers, nevertheless.

She had reason to be grateful for her parents' distraction as she reached her own room, took off the moist clothing and tucked herself into bed. Then she was remembering things she hadn't noticed at the time but which must have registered in her mind's eye: his pipe on the dressing-table next to her mother's pink curlers; a length of nylon twine coiled on the floor; the soft flame of a black candle; a magazine lying open on the pillow.

Then... Was it a week or so later? Who could absolutely care? Mother lugging a sledgehammer over to the shed, swinging it with the head just above the ground till its momentum at impact was sufficient to tear out the hook-and-eye he had on the inside and the door swung open to reveal him dressed in much the same way. At first it looked as if he was sitting down but then she and her mother realised that the rope connecting the apex of the shed roof and his neck was a couple of inches too short and that his backside wasn't actually in contact with the chair. His eyes were open wide but quite blind. He hadn't *intended* it to happen, that was the point, though her mother was doing all she could to make it look that way: removing all the magazines, then rushing to the house for some decent clothes in which to dress him before the ambulance arrived, by which time Mary was watching, as usual, from her bedroom window, other windows in the neighbourhood like eyes and her fingers reaching under her skirt to dance there in memorial.

Martin looks up as a fire-engine races up the street overtaking the line of other traffic, flecks of its blue light briefly across Beryl Cook's backyard and a snapshot of dark men in the cab fumbling with yellow helmets. Sometimes it's as if your breath would come easy for each and every China girl and no one else among these ruins of George Melly, music, the often mysterious procedures of strangers with coffee cups. In the café toilet, Mary rests the unwrapped tablet on her tongue till she senses the sedative quality beneath its coating, then swills it down her throat with sips of water from the brass tap, George's root-toots still pounding through the black-painted walls. Having pulled down her jeans and knickers she lightly rinses herself with wet fingers then sits on the white rim. *Not the seat. You never know who...* Looking down to where squashed-together thighs conceal most of it but still the familiar stinks of yesterday and the day before that and years lapping other years and the fingers and thumbs of unremembered conquistadors. Someone's written *I'll find him if it kills me* on the door, perhaps the briefest but most memorable theme ever expressed, a novella on a toilet door, a scrawl of immortality.

Ten minutes later, in the street, Martin is taking her hand and pulling her back from the kerb as a second fire-engine veers to this side of the road to avoid a broken-down bus. It's as if his fingers would love to plant the first seed of a vigorous mistletoe whose shoots would insinuate joint bank accounts, bobble-hat tea-cosies and fur-covered hot-water bottles. His hand maintains its grip as they finally run across, the sudden movement disturbing the stability of the cinema and the brown-and-yellow pub at its side.

'Somehow all this reminds me of Maurice Chevalier,' he's saying as they reach the other pavement. 'And though this may be the dimmest thing I've said so far, I'm really, you know, proud to be with you. And I wouldn't dream of being disrespectful to Rebecca (after all, I'm sure I have my drawbacks too) but I always wanted to take back-streets when we walked anywhere because, well, in my heart of hearts I wasn't proud. And if you're not proud then you're sunk. Still, that's all in the past. I'm proud now, that's the thing. Are you proud now?'

In the foyer they join a short queue of wax-jacket aesthetes and whereas it was once considered attractive to discuss such allegorical works prior to their showing in the hope of dissuading others you had come to devour any sexual content, this practice has recently been abandoned in favour of pretending you aren't going to see a film at all and for that reason it is necessary to comment on the weather, interest rates or the direction in which you're going to sail once your ship has come in. Martin croons over the illuminated sweet counter, humming towards the cellophane bags and waggling his hands in the pockets of his leather jacket. He'll have some of *those*, please; then he's calling to Mary, who's keeping their place in the queue, asking her if she fancies something and she's shaking her head though only once for fear of the foyer shaking with it. At a nod from the gentleman in the maroon suit who's been decorating the corner for some minutes, the queue begins to buy its tickets, then files (still in denial of being anywhere near a cinema) up the red-carpeted stairs to the circle or through double-doors to the groundlings. Martin hops to her side with a bag of Callard & Bowser; listens patiently to her declaration that the heights of the circle would be too much for her and even then that they must sit at the very back of the stalls, close to the double-doors. As far as Martin knows this is one of the last picture-houses in the city to retain its original layout and colour-scheme: a single large screen, threadbare seats, lofty rouge walls, a chandelier and acres of ornate plasterwork. Once inside, he takes her coat, folds it with his own, lays them on the empty seat next to him, then settles down to open his bag of toffees. On the screen is a still photo of a cigarette in an ashtray and beneath it the words *Patrons Are Reminded That This Is A No Smoking Auditorium* while the patrons themselves, coming gradually to the conclusion that they *are* in a cinema, choose to forget the reminder, and it is Martin's task to catch among conversations the occasional scratch and whisper of a match being lit, and the subsequent plumes of light blue smoke.

'You'll enjoy this,' he commands, holding the toffee bag under her nose. 'Go on. Have one. Do you good.'

She's already under siege from the EXIT sign to her left. 'No.'

'An ice-cream then?' He swings his bag towards a woman standing at the front of the stalls, a dimly lit tray at her waist.

'No, really.'

'Hey! I bet they do tubs. How about a tub? There was a time when I couldn't imagine going to the pictures without having a tub. Those little wooden spoons like squashed eights. Licking the ice-cream off the lid before you did anything else. Did you lick your lids? When I was small there weren't the flavours they have now. There was only one. Vanilla I suppose it was, only it wasn't called vanilla because there was no choice. It was just a tub. Go on, have one. Think of it as my treat.'

'No, honestly.'

The EXIT sign like a shiver in her perceptions, moving this way, that, looming forward, receding, jumping if she confines it to the corner of her eye. Matthew has told her a dozen times that these are symptoms to be expected. *They're just phantoms, after all, and phantoms can't do you any harm.* Well, no. His actual words were: 'They can do you no harm,' as if he'd spoken in a church from the wings of a brass eagle, the force of his incantations making him lose any commitment to apostrophe. 'They can do you no harm,' he said.

There's a run of advertisements, at first in still pictures accompanied by music which begins as if it is being wound up on a gramophone: waiters with silver trays (their smiles and jackets similar to those of the cinema manager) as symbols of some local Indian restaurant in which the cuisine is invariably *authentic;* young Palmolive couples smiling into the windows of shops selling diamond rings, which they'll purchase as symbolic hand-cuffs to guarantee their commitment to imminent misery; cheerfully clean motor mechanics with overalls full of belly tempting customers to have their car repaired at garages with alliterative names, this particular one being Mick's Motors. Subsequent advertisements comprise a standard piece of film with the name of a local shop or business tacked on to the end in blue, its rectangle usually out of true with the rest of the screen. Then something more expensive. A two-metre bottle of gin tipped by an invisible hand, the contents falling like twists of satin into a tumbler followed by the pink splash of an ice-cube and segment of lemon.

'Strawberry split, then? Quick, she'll be going in a minute.'

'No.'

Music from a barrel-organ accompanies a red-lipped woman in a cardboard hat (similar to the one worn by the woman in Stuffed Edwards) who slips on screen from the right, winks at the audience, tips back her head, opens her mouth and pokes into it the crinkled end of a sausage which protrudes from the end of a bun. Turning, Mary sees a fragment of green from the EXIT sign hanging against the surface of what must be moisture in Martin's eye. His knee falls against hers, shaking just a little.

As the woman folds her lips round this moistened foodstuff, Martin moves his mouth close to Mary's ear. 'This is the sort of thing I can't stand. Advertising hot-dogs when there aren't any on sale. I mean, watching that makes me really fancy one, doesn't it you? But there's none to be had.'

Mary's nodding.

'I reckon people should just go up and ask for one to see what kind of excuses the management have. It's a fat lot of good, isn't it, tempting you with something that doesn't exist?'

Mary continues to nod. 'Fat lot,' she says.

If you're unnerved by conversation, the easiest way round it is to repeat just a few words of the other person's speech; as with Matthew when, looking her in the eye he'd said, 'The alternative to recovery is that you go mad or die,' and all she'd been able to think of in reply was: *Go mad or die.*

She's fumbling with her cuffs, her legs poking into the aisle, a sense of repletion between them as if her jeans will soon give way and an unknown root will come chuckling upwards for her to smooth and soothe. A thump at the double-doors, then a silhouette tumbles down the aisle to the front of the stalls, rocking against the screen for a moment as it struggles with its coat before climbing into a seat. The ice-cream woman leans in its direction as she leaves, a finger to her lips. This velvet semi-darkness, the energetic EXIT sign, a tripping and teasing of signals to the brain, then the silhouette's voice bursts into a chorus of 'The Great Pretender', the sparse audience murmuring among itself at the resonance of this intruder – Martin too, his head now resting against hers.

'Always one, isn't there? Hell bent on ruining it for everyone else. And you can tell he's the kind of chap who'll bring the house down when Juanita and Julio... Well, you know. Funny, isn't it, this business with the Spanish and their Js? I'm not sure whether Jojoba beans come from Spain but it was a dead loss, wasn't it, having a shampoo ingredient with two soft Js? I mean, the British shopper's too shy to risk it so they probably opt for a shampoo they can pronounce even if they prefer the Jojoba one – see, I'm having trouble with it now. I'm of the opinion that if you want a British person to buy anything it should have lots of Ks in it. Soft Js are a washout. Oh, I wish that chap would be quiet. He'll ruin the start and there's quite a lot in the first few minutes you have to understand if the rest's going to make any sense.'

'You've seen it before then?'

Martin rearranges himself. 'Oh, no, no. It was in that write-up I mentioned on the phone. Apparently the council tried to get it banned locally. Something about tomatoes, but don't worry, it's not rude or anything. Anyway, don't people make a fuss about you know what? They'll watch car bombs in Beirut while they're stuffing themselves with waffles but anything to do with, well, sex and everything, and they're up in arms. I would have thought it should be the other way round. I mean, if I saw car bombs going off in the street every day I probably wouldn't take much notice of them on the TV. And what's more natural, tell me, than a man and woman, you know...?'

The screen yawns to make way for an opening shot of a Spanish landscape across which roam several yards of credits to snatches of Flamenco music alternating with a dry silence broken only by the rattle of cicadas.

'I've always wanted to know what a key grip does,' whispers Martin.

He's sighing as if very tired, each intake and exhalation of breath instigating a mechanism which somehow contrives to crackle his Callard & Bowsers.

'And I don't believe that one, for a start. Did you see it? Lighting director – Juan Thomas?'

The auditorium has darkened further. Mary traps a hand between her thighs, their moisture against her thumb.

'I hope you don't mind me bringing this up, Mary, but I'm beginning to feel like sixteen all over again. I mean it's not so bad getting older and throwing off that ... that slough of anachronisms – how about that one! – but all the same, isn't it nice now and then not to bother with knowing the facts so you can lie back and hanker after the exhilarations of – well, adolescence I suppose you'd call it. Those times you thought would never end when there were long summer afternoons, snow at Christmas, and unrequited love for the girl in the bike sheds who didn't like you a bit and then that ... that blind determination to solve the troubles of the world. Toffee?'

With her free hand Mary grips the seat in front of her as if to counteract threats from the precipitous walls, the relentless EXIT sign. All of them stupid things, as is the faint whine of another siren in the street, but if each persists she'll cry, or something worse. The sights and sounds may be invading her bloodstream, poisoning its regular function.

A crumpling of the bag in Martin's hand. 'Toffee?'

'No.'

'Well, look. Just reach across if you want one. I'll leave them here. They're very good. I don't eat them normally but I like to do something a bit different when I come to the pictures. If you do the same as you would normally do, then a night like this is harder to remember, don't you think? Not that I'm insinuating I wouldn't remember this one anyway. I mean, with you here, how could I ever, well...'

Crackle as the bag settles in his lap.

'There are some marvellous opening scenes. Just you see this.'

'You *have* seen it before.'

'No, really. It was just another thing Montague Parrish mentioned in that write-up, now I come to think of it.'

'Maybe we should have stayed in and watched *that*.'

'Teasing me, aren't you? No, the write-up was an appetiser, nothing more. Montague Parrish — everyone calls him MP — always gets it right. In fact, I've heard quite a few people say they don't go to a film unless he's given them the nod, so to speak. I saw him in Allied Carpets the other week. He wears terrific hats.'

'Was Bamber with him?'

'And it struck me straight away that he was the sort of chap who looks *right* in a hat. Some men can get away with it. Some can't. And if you can't, it doesn't matter what sort of hat you try or what you do with your hair, it still won't look right. Old Montague was born for hats, just as he seemed born for the shin-length leather coat. George Melly – the one we heard in the café – he looks good in a hat. But if you accept this point of view you'd have to conclude that I'm a non-hat person. Women don't have the problem so much because, as a rule, they look, well, delightful in a hat. It adds to them. If I wore a hat people would laugh because I haven't a ... a hat mentality.'

The camera's panning to a run-down stone-built bar, the cameraman, as it were, pushing through swing-doors to a room full of tables where a perspiring, unshaven Clint Eastwood figure sits with a bottle and pulls a penknife through the flesh of a peach.

'It's the man from Del Monte,' calls the drunk from the front of the stalls.

The juices of Martin's intestinal system flush through one constriction after another, provoking him to tap his abdomen with a clenched fist or apologise with dim eyebrows to Mary as she deals unsuccessfully with the dancing of the chandelier high above the uninvited images of men on vertiginous stepladders painting the plasterwork; and as the men lean back to inspect their work, so she jumps in her seat and so the images repeat themselves. She's been trying to find a harmless place to look, one which would avoid both the EXIT sign and a direct confrontation with the screen where the stubbled someone flops across the table, his peach rolling to the floor, where it's trapped by the toe of a black shoe belonging, perhaps, to Jaunita. Ignoring this drama, other patrons of the bar share jokes with a matronly figure standing behind the counter. Martin laughs to himself because he's been reading the subtitles. If you're meant to find a particular moment amusing, the subtitle has an exclamation mark, though the drunk in the stalls appears oblivious to this convention, laughing whether there is an exclamation mark or not.

'The chap lying on the table's Julio,' says Martin. 'At least, I think it might be.'

She's trying to deepen her breathing, but it's as if each and every piece of advice offered by Matthew induces a keener sense of unease. Martin throws himself backwards in delight at some aesthetic *double-entendre* she's missed, then nudges her with his elbow, his lips unzipped. She nods. He jerks his chin to the left. She picks at the back of the red seat. His teeth soften another Callard & Bowser. *Martin's busy day.* No sooner has he swallowed than his fingers are crackling through the bag for another and the music of his juices is heightened by the one being currently digested. He twists a paper wrapper till the auditorium itself unwinds.

'You really should try a toffee. The mint ones are fabulous. They remind me of my grandmother. She wasn't happy unless she had one in her mouth. Kept them in a Chinese tobacco jar by her armchair. Dr Kildare, a glass of lemonade and a mint toffee, and she was in heaven. There are whole generations of kids growing up who won't know grandmothers like I had. The traditional sort, I mean. All wax floors and commandments. Church on Sundays. Fruit cake. Hats like upturned soup tureens. She used to say to me, "Mart, keep God in your head, bread in your tummy and a tool in your hand and you won't go far wrong." Let her down on the tool bit, but then she wasn't to know the country would go down the tube or that those of us with O-levels would be drowning in an ocean of chaps with degrees in this and that. I'm sure that's why it was easier to be famous in the old days when ninety-nine per cent of the country were absolute dumbos, making it a cinch for people like old Priestley to shine through. Wouldn't stand a chance now, would he? Probably be buttering Sunblest in a sandwich bar. These days you keep climbing but the mountain keeps getting higher, don't you think? A kind of intellectual inflation out of control. I'm not being disrespectful, at least I don't think I am, but people like my grandmother had, well, minimal expectations. And let's face it, she didn't crack up, take pills or sleep around. Sorry. Practically lived off beef-dripping. And if I'd have said to her, "Grummy" – that's what we called her – "Grummy, I'm feeling a lot of stress," she'd have given me a clip round the ear. And though I'm naturally pleased to be living in a world of so-called opportunity where I can buy pre-cooked beef in airtight packets any time of the day, I often regret – as if regret was in my chromosomes – the passing of an age in which it was possible for Grummies to put their feet up on Sunday afternoons and for people like Miss Marple to ride in those big green cars with the straps round the bonnet and where men were decent chaps in open-necked shirts who wouldn't say boo to a goose till they had to shoot someone from another country to protect the mother-land. I mean, I don't believe in war, but can you imagine some of those pale-faced financial advisers beating off the Japs with the bonnets of their XR3s? Sorry, something's got into me. I think it's you. I can feel you next to me even when I'm not looking and it's as if I've just been let out of an attic after a very long time. I want to talk and talk, introduce you to how I really am, let you see the man behind the – well, mask I suppose, though I've never thought of myself as wearing one. The strange, contradictory thing is that a chap doesn't fare too well if he doesn't have a mask, but I've cut my losses and been careful not to wear one. And it's what I love about you, that you haven't got one on either. You're just as nature intended and I *like* that.'

Beige shadows over a parched landscape as Julio staggers outside, gazes through puffed eyes at the sun and then, to the strumming of a guitar, expels the contents of his stomach, his hand resting on the patterned blanket-saddle of a mule tied to a post, which shuffles to one side. In close-up, the ruined peach lands in the dust at his feet. He swings round to see Juanita at the bar entrance, her hands tight against her waist, a curl of disgust in one corner of her mouth. He's simply an actor, this bile some coloured porridge retained in his mouth till the director told him to cough it out, yet Mary turns away from the screen to see clearly – but in silhouette – the drunk lifting a bottle to his lips. She's plucking at the moist seam of her jeans, introducing blooms of quietness to a system in revolt. The manager pads down the aisle, has a quiet word with the silhouette, then pads to the back again, the floor creaking under his black shoes as he settles himself into a shadow beside the double-doors.

'Pssst. Forgive me but you're most beautiful in this light. I know I should shut up but something comes over me and I'm, well, hopeless. If a spirit were to come along now and say I could have nothing more than this – the pictures, a few toffees and you – I think I'd be reasonably contented. I'm afraid my ambitions at this time are virtually nil. Close to you like this, I have a yawning sensation within and each yawn sends a quickening through my veins. Whenever it happens I think to myself, "Martin, what more could you possibly want?" What's with this world which must have this and must have that? Remember being young when you'd come home after playing in the snow with your fingers dead and your scarf soaked through, and all you wanted was to be warm and have some triangles of buttered toast? Well, that's more or less how I feel. My life has been a winter's day and you must be the...'

Mary was following Billy the Boot as he explained his theory that Nat King Cole was unsuited to the attentions of women and though the bones of the theory held substance, her head, requiring distraction without reference to feeling, was singing 'Unforgettable'. They were on their way to the room of a friend of

his who'd got hold of some really magic stuff. She remembers a
man in a trilby bumping into Billy on the street, receiving two
fingers for his trouble and stopping to relate the tale to a knot of
elderly ladies standing by the window of an electrical shop where
Prince Charles was doing something official on ranks of television sets. The Prince's hat had feathers and he was wearing a
sword. She was trying to think it through – why some people had
hats with feathers and a sword at their hip while others didn't.
Then Billy was leading her through a partially stripped door into
a room with black and silver walls where strangers were curling
up on stained beanbags surrounded by records without sleeves,
empty beer-cans, tins of baked beans with raised lids and parts of
a motorcycle engine, the chain hanging out of a dish of paraffin.

'Brought a friend along,' said Billy the Boot. He and Mary had
some of the really magic stuff. In the corner was a violet bed and
on it a tall woman in leather was shaking her head to Led
Zeppelin ... Mary laughing and unbearably ticklish as several of
the clientele helped her out of her jeans and jumper and lay her
beside the leather woman. For a while everyone was swapping
stories, but then a bright light came on and three of the men
were climbing to their feet, the middle one holding some sort of
camera on his shoulder and the leather woman running her glove
along Mary's leg, everyone wild and having a fine time of it,
especially when one of the other men helped her with her
underwear. Billy was grinning from his beanbag, his arms
folded, saying, 'See, I told you, you bastards. Didn't I tell you?'
Then the woman's glove being peeled off, falling to the floor, and
Mary almost doubled up with the tickle of the red-nailed hand,
turning her head away from the bright light because it was
hurting her eyes. A man at each ankle, the camera reaching
through music and back again... The ceiling, she remembers,
was covered in painted tiles as the woman unzipped her zips one
by one and ended up crouched over Mary's breasts but backwards

to cheers from the ankle men and applause from Billy the Boot till it was the woman's turn to hold an ankle, freeing each of the men in turn to come hunting, Billy the Boot last of all, and quite suddenly the music was changing to the Beatles. *There are places I remember, all my life, though some have changed.* She'd been in love with Lennon once and if anyone cared to ask her then she would have said her favourite lyric of all time was 'Imagine'. By then the camera was trying to get a good shot of the woman's tongue and Mary was up to her knees in back-streets, Billy helping her along the pavement till finally his legs gave way and he collapsed against a pile of bricks, taking her with him but laughing anyway. 'What a crazy fucking afternoon,' said Billy the Boot, climbing to his feet by grabbing the side of a skip. 'You were absolutely lunatic.' And she was still laughing as she tried to get up but fell in a heap at Billy's feet, forcing him to pull her along by her jumper, his voice cracking around the warehouse walls. Later, the glitter of a boating pond, a buffed brass band thumping at its edge, and as she ran she was remembering summers and the loss of them, Billy at the top of the rise calling to her but she kept running till he was out of sight.

An end to the splashing of toffee between Martin's teeth. On the screen Julio has decapitated a rival with such speed and eloquence that the dying lips are still moving as his head rolls through the dust. Julio picks up the head by its hair, holding it at arm's length as a signal to Juanita that he's rather fond of her. Sickened yet exhilarated, she's beckoning him towards a building in the background and, having winked at his rival, Julio swings round, throws the head as far as he can, then stomps through the dust in pursuit of Juanita, wiping blood from his fingers on to his shirt. The drunk at the front of the stalls has got to his feet, shaking his fist and voicing his approval, prompting the manager to unhook himself from the door-shadow, pad down the aisle in the crimson manner unique to his profession and say in a loud whisper, 'I'm very sorry, sir, but I'm afraid you'll have to leave now.'

'Yeah, chuck the bastard out,' yells an aesthete from the gloom.

A struggle of silhouettes, a flapping of coat, the manager assisting the drunk into the aisle, light from his torch flashing against the man's thick spectacles...

'How dare you eject innocent persons from places of entertainment.'

'That's exactly what I'm doing, sir. Now come quietly and we won't have to call the police.'

A bottle falling to the floor. 'Oh bring them all if you must. Every last one of them.'

A 'Tsk' from Martin as Juanita pokes a huge key into the lock, turns it and, with another glance at Julio, kicks open the door.

The bag appears under Mary's nose.

'This is your last chance,' whispers Martin. 'There's banana or ordinary.'

She's picking one but leaving it unwrapped in her palm, where it grows soft. The walls take on a certain weight and menace. From the foyer come muffled cries, the thump of a chair perhaps against a wall. Mingling with the blue projected light and the angers of an EXIT sign there's a perfume, a smell of fictions, China girl leaning against the parapet of an imaginary bridge on some green afternoon, the wind childish with her hair and the full fluency of her expression visible from a hiding place among the bushes. She's been having a gentle day through the beech trees, pausing where rock pokes through turf, listening to voices along the stream far below, being the confidante to her own secrets. Another memory, one of Mary's own, not made up, of an isle somewhere, and she's standing on the white cliff above an ink sea, a swell of headland to her right on which (the guidebook says) poets once walked; then later a soft churchyard, where she wandered past rows of silent witnesses whose last home lay beneath hawthorn shade and rumours of sea wind. At the far end, sitting on a wall, a young woman was looking over the meadow towards a scrap of sea. Mary's meanwhile squeezing fingers between her jeans as in a small room stacked with boxes of tomatoes, Julio's hand hooks round Juanita's waist, her mouth unleashing words of anger at him, but finally pushing against his. Martin coughs, crossing his legs as the screen splits into eight rectangles, each with a different perspective of the couple as they undress and fall to a dirt floor soon strewn with ruined tomatoes. As each rectangle regularly changes places with one of the other seven, it's difficult to follow the minutiae of love-making though Martin, leaning forward to rest his elbows on the seat in front, does his best. This is the sense of death and being born again, the letting go of nightmares in favour of ordinary dreams, her heart pumping less quickly but still weighing heavily, her palms moist, a prickling on the undersurface of her skull. The sunburnt roll of Juanita's body crushes tomatoes first in one rectangle then in another, so piss to his incantations and was that Julio's penis? His buttocks burst a tomato; or, there, seeds dribbling over Juanita's thigh while, to the left, Julio grinds a tomato between her legs till its skin yields and its pulp trickles into her pubic hair; or her lips suckle his thick fingers ... Martin fumbles in his bag for the last Callard & Bowser. Juanita's nipple is wet with juice and the webs of Julio's saliva as it springs from his mouth. Yes, it was his penis – it's over there now, comparatively small in terms of the rest of him and abysmally limp as they always are in films, everyone asked to go along with falsehoods which is why, despite the rapture, one didn't glimpse Sutherland's in *Don't Look Now*. If this film weren't fiction, Juanita and Julio would be lying in the dark with lighted cigarettes discussing his impotence, but for now they're rolling over tomatoes, the trunks-shaped un-sunburnt patch of Julio's backside pumping between Juanita's legs while, adjacent to this, their mouths begin a joint assault on the largest tomato; then the two of them top to toe, Juanita smothering Julio's thighs in pulp and he, invisibly, suckling somewhere near her middle; and in the top right corner, both lubricated by the light orange tomato flesh, Juanita, her hands backwards against the floor, slips her wet buttocks over Julio's abdomen till her pubis almost reaches his hidden penis. ('Ah, the allegory's unfolding,' whispers Martin.) And here's Julio standing astride Juanita's thighs, crushing tomatoes in his hands, the juice and pulp splashing to her abdomen. A world of tomatoes and their consequences, their residue coagulating on the dirt floor, adhering to these naked bodies, a rapture of fruits.

Mary reaches for her coat. 'Think I'll be going now.'

'Sorry?'

'I'm going.'

Martin unravels his coat from hers. 'Yeah, you're right. This is pretty disgusting, isn't it?'

'It's not that. I just don't like it in here. I don't feel too good.'

Juanita in praise of Julio, kneeling before him, hands to his hips, her head moving back and forth. Julio in praise of Juanita, her legs hooked over his shoulders, his hands supporting her back, his mouth supposedly sipping her. Julio behind Juanita as she rests on all fours, his thick hands pressed to the fruits of her backside, traces of tomato along the length of her spine, a microphone picking up the slap of his skin against hers.

'Yes, let's go. These aesthetic principle films are two a penny. It's criminal anyway. Just think what the Third World could do with all those tomatoes.'

Mary glances back as the screen becomes one again fully to capture the last moments of love-making, Julio's hands upon Juanita's back as she rolls above him, reaching for climax.

Martin puts on his coat, then drapes Mary's round her shoulders, the weight of his lips in her hair. Juanita's crying out

and they're coming through the double-doors into the fluorescent foyer, the manager picking up Smartie tubes which have
fallen to the floor.

'She's not too well,' explains Martin to the woman knitting in
the ticket booth. The ticket woman nods. The foyer hums, and
following the rawness of Spain it's a shock to tap down marble
steps into a cold street, Mary quite sick of insubstantiality and
sicker still of inward focus as Martin leads her along the grey
pavement. The street has emptied somewhat, though it roars
periodically with youngsters in sports cars or horns reprimanding
careless pedestrians. A sky cracks with night-fatigue as they pass
the takeaways, wine bars, couples in delicate conversation. It's
good to imagine them together day by day, good to think of
them reading newspapers or washing down a second-hand car.
It's as if there's never an end to movement and as if it'll be a
salvation some time in the future, this refusal to stop. Martin's
asking her to wait where she is while he goes into the off-licence.
With hands against her jeans she can sense the outline of it lying
there, in hibernation as it were, though it begins to stir once
more as she trails a fingertip along its length. A jangle of the
doorbell, Martin waggling a bottle of wine or, as he calls it,
'Dutch Courage'. Moments later they're passing a shop whose
window is dominated by a large portrait of Jesus on the cross.
The window has been otherwise emptied to enhance its stature.
The portrait has a plastic frame though the surface of the canvas
or whatever has been especially created to have a three-dimensio-
nal effect as you pass, the eyes of Jesus one moment looking
down, the next flickering at you as if to say: *And where do you think
you're going?* Martin stoops, leans sideways, looms upwards
saying, 'I wondow how they do that?' before losing interest and
putting his arm round her. She glances back as they carry on to
see Jesus still watching her. 'It's all very well,' Martin's saying,
'but it was thirty-five pounds. And to my way of thinking,

though Jesus might be pleased to have himself put into three
dimensions, I think he'd be a trifle irritated at having a price. Do
you know what I mean? Like when you have to pay to look round
cathedrals. I'd *hate* that if I was Jesus. Still, that's enough of *Him*.
I've been thinking about you and it's a bit like the first day of
spring in here.' He's tapping his heart with the side of the wine-
bottle. 'Yes, spring – the day you wake to the perfumes of a new
season or spot your first bluebell in a wood. Then I keep thinking
about the things which could have got in the way of our meeting
at the castle. I'd have, well, gone round the twist if this had all
turned out to be another trick of fantasy. Isn't living ... isn't
living a curious, unpredictable, patchwork thing, like dishwater
for days on end till, Twing! – there's a vision, a moment of
music, a resurrection of the mystical.'

Above the rooftops further along there's a contest of emergency lights and, against the sky, palls of orange-tinted smoke
obscuring the cold stars. She'll be saving the memory of China
girl's mouth till last of all, unfolding it like a secret note on the
threshold of sleep.

'And I'd do anything for you, though I can imagine others
saying, "Don't be so ridiculous, Martin." But what do they
know? It's a hobby of some people to slander nice things – *nice*
things – having a hand to hold, for example; someone who won't
mind that you lose sleep over nothings at all or fret over the
possibility of death from things in the lungs or things in the sky.
Yeah, someone *nice* with nothing up their sleeve. You're nice.
Nice as pie and I'm chuffed to bits. And even if you were the only
one I felt like this about, I'd be happy. I'm not a fool, you know –
I realise things change and that feelings, well, mature and stuff,
but some people *have* to keep reminding you of it with grins on
their faces as if they were looking forward to the day you have to
queue in a post office on a Wednesday with lines of wet
pensioners. Being contented and expectant has had a bad press,

you know. Misery is supposedly the key to success. Yes, I'd be happy with you. To have it proven just once that there's something more than all this.' He sweeping his arm in an arc across the city. 'Sorry.'

Across the street, men and women are on their way to a *Rocky Horror Show*, both sexes dressed in stockings and basques, the ones towards the front making hypothetical jokes while those at the rear look back periodically to the scene of the emergency as if guilty of carrying on their good time with fire-engines about.

'And in one sense I'm grateful you're under the weather because it gives me a chance to look after you, even if it doesn't last long. And don't you find anyway that people who've been under the weather have more of a spirituality about them? Sometimes it's good to live with the thought of a gun to your head so you can see the value of things you normally, well, take for granted.' He pats her shoulder. 'Don't worry about all that up ahead, it won't be anything to do with us. And as for images, well, I've never had one. Funny, but everywhere you go, you're asked to deal with them, images; images you're supposed to relate to by comparing them with a mental file you have of familiar ones. Perhaps it's something to do with these *Rocky Horror* fans. I've heard people say they daren't go to one of the shows in ordinary get-up, and that's a bit like the world in reverse. *You* don't have an image either which is why I... But the point is, I don't care a scrap for people you can predict. I prefer the challenge of learning new meanings for old signals. Are you following this or am I being a prat?'

Madness to answer him each time he asks a question since he's simply hewing false destinies from a fictional plan he's contrived and now unconfidently applauds it as Mary, worn out, rests against his arm and looks ahead to the flashing police car which has been parked across the end of her road to prevent other traffic getting in. Yes, pillows of smoke-stained blue and orange are mushrooming above the roofs, the familiar crackles of burning wood, sparks drifting skyward, Martin's unremarkable legs swinging relentlessly, a group of three of four other *Rocky Horrors* waving beer-cans, exaggerating masculine strides to ridicule their own clothing and how can they stand it in this sudden raw with the first twinkles of frost on the road? Couples, heads down, over the zebra crossing; the busy late-night supermarket and a beautiful woman tying up her two collies outside and wagging her finger at them; a stranger resting against the purple walls of the gothic library; the hush of soft paper round the wine-bottle in Martin's hand; and from a dormer window in the building next to the tyre depot, trickles of song and conversation from silhouettes.

Scratching to remember. It can't have been much more than a day or two later when she heard similar wood-crackling through her bedroom window and looked out to see her father's shed just a phantom among sheets of flame, and her mother standing well back, her arms folded. Neighbours, not being able to distinguish between accident and design, had called the fire brigade but when they finally came her mother told them she'd been trying to clear some rubbish, that was all. They warned her not to be so careless in future, especially with something as big as *that*. Sparks could have fallen into a dozen other things, including someone else's home. By then the heavy roar of fire had eased; the roof and walls had fallen in and what remained was burning in a less dramatic way. Next morning there was a mound of brittle cinders with a crimson core, lengths of scorched but otherwise intact wood surrounding them. Her mother was up early. Still in her nightdress, she was hauling unburnt pieces of wood into the crimson with a rake till they became cinders too. Later still, she dug a hole and buried them.

Well, the smell of things like that hangs in the memory and it's one of the reasons living must be *considered* – because of what may later hang there. Martin's protecting her with his arm as if he's just come true as the fantasy of himself, his insides beating for her, steeled for the challenge she represents, eager to study each corpuscle of her till Kingdom (or whatever cruel things) come.

At the corner of her road, a small group of people are being kept from the immediate scene by a policeman. She sees Mrs Charles from next door and, at the front, China girl in her white dressing-gown as firemen come and go through the front door of the elderly person's house, its lower windows blackened and cracked, smoke billowing through broken upper windows, the black-and-yellow men in breathing apparatus and, all across the road, a tangle of hosepipes, pieces of charred furniture, the crusts of a mattress. A few yards further along is an ambulance, its engine running, hazard-lights yellowing other windows. A second policeman stands by the driver's door, a helmet in his hand. Most of the students are leaning out of their own windows, one of them with a camera. *Far and few, far and few are the lands where the...* China girl – her arms folded, hair crisp and beautiful against white cotton, her slim body stiff with cold; and Martin – just here, unable to say much, guilty as anything with his passion and his bottle of wine. *Jumblies live.* Waiting. Waiting some more till the policeman persuades the group there's nothing more to see and everyone should move along. China girl heads slowly for the steps, hopping here and there over hosepipes. She has immaculate oriental slippers. As usual she skips up to the door, her hair skipping with her, so completely beautiful and perhaps it's the weight of Mary's gaze on the back of her neck which prompts her to turn at the last moment, spot her with Martin and wave. Mary could cry with the resonance of it, beauty. The door slams. Martin won't take his arm from her shoulder; is keeping his lips tight together and an indelicate frown on his forehead to avoid accusations of good cheer in a grim situation. From China girl's living-room window, a brief glimpse of her white face, then darkness. Mary's twisting the key, kicking open the door. In the hall Martin pretends to yawn, takes off his coat, lays it on the table as a signal of togetherness, unwinds the tissue paper and holds up his bottle of wine.

'Um, perhaps you could get a couple of glasses. I'd quite like to, well ... I need to have a bit of a chat.'

He's wandering into what has become *his* living room, sitting on the sofa, rolling the wine-bottle in his hands.

'You wait there, I won't be a minute,' she says, going into her bedroom, lying down and for a while giving way to tears of whatever it is: relief, gratitude, love perhaps, but then a more easily understood sensation is sparked by stray fingers beneath her hips, persuading her to wipe her eyes and stand at ease in front of the wardrobe mirror. She's tugging off her coat, jumper, blouse and bra, twirling once and shaking with cold; unbuttoning her jeans, pulling them down, yanking each leg of them away from her feet, then slipping off her socks before tearing her knickers with one firm pull and throwing the rag of them aside. She'll draw back the curtains, watch the couple in the sky sipping from mugs at their table, having what must be an idle conversation at the end of another day. And the thing of it is, they're *still* leading extraordinary lives, finely attuned in matching magnolia dressing-gowns, his longest finger waggling the tip of her nose and she wriggling with the fun of it. This time it is he who grows impatient, stands up and indicates with jerks of the head he's ready for bed with her, yet she accedes to it with less of a struggle than he may have done, letting her gown fall to the floor as she follows him through to the bedroom, both lights going out. *The owl and the pussycat went to sea.* Leaving her curtains open and light off, Mary reaches upwards with her fingertips in a protracted yawn in which her body arches backwards, delineating each fold, crease and shadow, each trace of muscle and bone beneath faint green skin, her hands falling naturally then to where the sense of it rears diagonally, kinked slightly towards the tip, and she hears Martin's shoes tapping out of sight against the hall tiles because he's been unable to wait where he was told to, thinking she may have hung herself, escaped, or worse. But she's lying in front of the wardrobe mirror, her knees pressed to the mahogany at either side, her head raised, fingers one moment cherishing its length, the next slipping into lips at either side, easing them apart to examine traces of blood, this glutinous moisture, her readiness for recovery from the dark, the flesh at her abdomen and breast silvered by broad moonlight falling through the window, in her throat and oesophagus the nausea of uncertainty changing to a nausea of *wanting*. Wet fingers playing here, there, in each crease of skin, each shadow, each mound or fold of hair and all the while the tap of Martin's shoes or an impatient sigh. From upstairs the lyric of China girl who's maybe early to bed with a book, a glass of lemon water and sweet talcum toes men have dreams of taking in their mouths ... *went to sea in a beautiful pea-green boat.*

'Hello? Mary? What about these drinks? I was hoping that we could, well, sit together and have a nice ... chat, you know, *together.*'

She's twisting this way and that in her secrecy, dreaming fresh perspectives of it, catching it in various moments of moonlight, her waist undulating as seductive as a snake in branches, more strands of hair than earlier, surely, at the fringes of her aureoles and this transluscent membrane yielding to the stiffness of tissue beneath.

'Fuck the drinks,' she's saying. 'I want you to come in here. *Now.*'

A purple silence.

'You mean...?'

'Absolutely.'

She hears the slap of his palm against the hall wall. 'Ah, well, you see that's really what I wanted to talk to you about. I've told you I want this to be an honest relationship – if we're having one, that is – so I ought to tell you...' Oh for goodness sake, Martin '... to be frank with you, you're the first woman I've...'

She's dribbling on to her finger to moisten its journey around the imaginary tip.

'... and I didn't think it would, well, come to this so soon. Ha! I'm a bit scared, to tell you the truth. You musn't laugh, promise? Only I haven't *done it* before. Not fully anyway. I've kissed, with Rebecca, but something, you know, always held me back. In fact I haven't even seen a woman with ... with no clothes on except at the pictures and places like that. Not in reality.'

It seems the tissue beneath her fingers stiffens inexorably as, with a suppleness and agility she's never known before, her thighs roll backwards over her head and her mouth comes within inches of victory.

'Then come and take a good look,' she laughs.